查姆

张永祥 选编
郭思九 陶学良 整理
杨柳 译
[美]H.W.Lan 审校

“十三五”国家重点图书
中国南方民间文学典籍英译丛书
丛书主编 张立玉 丛书副主编 起国庆

CHAMU

出品单位：
中南民族大学南方少数民族文库翻译研究基地

WUHAN UNIVERSITY PRESS
武汉大学出版社

·汉英对照·

图书在版编目(CIP)数据

查姆:汉英对照/张永祥选编;杨柳译.—武汉:武汉大学出版社,2021.12

中国南方民间文学典籍英译丛书/张立玉主编

“十三五”国家重点图书

ISBN 978-7-307-22667-8

Ⅰ.查… Ⅱ.①张… ②杨… Ⅲ.彝族—史诗—中国—汉、英 Ⅳ.I222.7

中国版本图书馆 CIP 数据核字(2021)第 212979 号

责任编辑:罗晓华　　责任校对:李孟潇　　版式设计:韩闻锦

出版发行:**武汉大学出版社**　(430072　武昌　珞珈山)

(电子邮箱:cbs22@whu.edu.cn　网址:www.wdp.whu.edu.cn)

印刷:湖北恒泰印务有限公司

开本:720×1000　1/16　　印张:17　　字数:205 千字

版次:2021 年 12 月第 1 版　　2021 年 12 月第 1 次印刷

ISBN 978-7-307-22667-8　　定价:48.00 元

丛书编委会

序

近年来，民族典籍英译捷报频传，硕果累累。韩家全教授等人的壮族系列经典翻译陆续出版，王宏印教授等人的系列民族典籍英译研究著作已经问世，李正栓教授等人的藏族格言诗英译著作不断在国内外出版，王维波教授等人的东北民族典籍英译著作纷纷付梓，李昌银教授等人的“云南少数民族经典作品英译文库”于2018年年底出版，其他民族典籍英译作品也在接踵而至。

近日，中南民族大学张立玉教授传来佳音：他们要出版“十三五”国家重点图书——“中国南方民间文学典籍英译丛书”。虽叫民间文学，其实基本上都是民族典籍。这一系列包括十本书，它们是《黑暗传》《哭嫁歌》《哈尼阿培聪坡坡》《彝族民间故事》《南方民间创世神话选集》《查姆》《召树屯》《娥并与桑洛》《金笛》《梅葛》。其中，好几本是云南少数民族的。只有一本是汉族典籍，即《黑暗传》。很有意思的是，这些典籍展示了不同民族的创世史诗或诸如此类的东西。

《黑暗传》以民间歌谣唱本形象地描述了盘古开天辟地结束混沌黑暗、人类起源及社会发展的历程，融合了混沌、盘古、女娲、伏羲、炎帝神农氏、黄帝轩辕氏等众多英雄人物在洪荒时代艰难创世的一系列神话传说。它被称为汉族首部创世史诗。《哈尼阿培聪坡坡》是一部完整地记载哈尼族历史沿革的长篇史诗，堪称哈尼族的“史记”，长5000余行，以现实主义手法记叙了哈尼族祖先在各个历史时期的迁徙情况，并对其迁徙各地的原因、路线、途程，各个迁居地的社会生活、生产、风习、宗教，以及与毗邻民族的关系等，均作了详细而生动的辑录，因而该作品不仅具有文学价值，而且具有重大的历史学、社会学及宗教学价值。《南方民间创世神话选集》包括一些创世神话，主要是关于世界起源和人类起源的神话。本书所列包括生活在广泛地域的民族，如门巴族、珞巴族、怒族、基诺族、普米族、拉祜族、傈僳族、毛南族、德昂族、景颇族、阿昌族、布朗族、佤族、独龙族、水族、仡佬族、布依族、仫佬族、高山族和侗族等。这些神话不仅讲述了世界的起源，也讲述了人类的始祖，以及人类对世界的改造。《梅葛》是彝族的一部长篇史诗，流传在云南省楚雄州的姚安、大姚等彝族地区。“梅葛”本为一种彝族歌调的名称，由于人们采用这种调子来唱彝族的创世史，因而创世史诗被称为“梅葛”。《查姆》是一部彝族史诗，是彝族人民唱天地、日月、人类、种子、风雨、树木等起源的长篇史诗，被彝族人民当作本民族的历史来看待。

其余几本书展示了一些少数民族的风俗习惯、恋爱故事、斗争故事等。《哭嫁歌》是土家族文化典籍。“哭嫁”是土家族姑娘在出嫁时进行的一种用歌声来诉说自己在封建买办婚姻制度下不幸命运的活动，是指土家族姑娘的抒情歌谣，富有诗韵和乐感，融哀、怨、喜和乐为一体，以婉转的曲调向世人展示土家人独特的“哭”文化。《彝族民间故事》是一部以流传于云南楚雄彝族自治州彝族人民中间的民间故事为主体，同时覆盖全省包括小凉山等彝族地区的民间故事集。这些故事丰富多彩，从中能看到民族民间故事的各种形态和生动、奇妙而颇具彝族民族特色的文化特征。《召树屯》是傣族民间长篇叙事诗，叙述了傣族佛教世俗典籍《贝叶经·召树屯》中一个古老的传说故事。这部叙事诗一直为傣族人民所传唱，历久不衰。《娥并与桑洛》是一部优美生动的叙事诗，一个凄美的爱情悲剧。《金笛》是一部苗族长篇叙事诗，富于变幻性和传奇性，尽情铺叙扎董丕冉与蒙诗彩奏的悲欢离合，热情赞颂他们在与魔虎的激烈斗争中所表现出来的坚贞不屈、英勇顽强的精神，许多情节含有浓郁的民族特色。

这些故事都很引人入胜，都很符合国家文化发展需求，向世人讲述中国故事，传播中华文化，并且讲述的是民族故事，充分体现了党和国家对各民族的关怀。

民族典籍英译是传播中国文化、文学和文明的重要途径，是中华文化"走出去"的重要组成部分，是国家战略，是提高文化"软实力"的重要方式，在文化交流和文明建设中起着不可或缺的作用，对提升中国国际话语权和构建中国对外话语体系以及对建设世界文学都有积极意义。

中国民族典籍使世界文化更加丰富多彩、绚丽多姿。我国各民族典籍中折射出的文化多样性极大地丰富了世界多元、特色鲜明的文化。人们对多样性形成全新的认识角度和思维方式，有助于开阔视野，丰富思考问题的角度，挖掘这些经典中的教育价值和文化价值，对世界其他民族都有指导和借鉴意义，并且有助于建设我国的文化自信。

民族典籍翻译与研究事业关乎国家的稳定统一，关乎民族关系的和谐发展，关乎世界多元文化的实现。在中国，民族典籍资源极为丰富，有待进一步挖掘、翻译，仍有许多少数民族典籍亟待拯救，民族典籍翻译与研究工作任重而道远，民族典籍翻译事业大有可为。

李正栓①

2019年7月19日

---

① 李正栓，中国英汉语比较研究会典籍英译专业委员会常务副会长兼秘书长；中国中医药研究促进会传统文化翻译与国际传播专业委员会常务主任委员。

前　言

享誉海内外的彝族创世史诗《查姆》被称为彝族的“根谱”，它是一部流传于云南楚雄双柏县大麦地镇、安龙堡乡等地区的彝族民间文学创世史诗，在彝族发展的历史长河中逐步形成并流传下来。它经历了口耳相传，经过彝族人一代代的传递，最终以彝文手抄本的形式流传在楚雄彝族自治州的部分地区。

《查姆》是“云南民族民间文学典藏”系列之一。它以神话传说的方式，记述了人类、万物的起源和发展历史，是彝族人民唱天地、日月、人类、种子、风雨、树木等起源的长篇史诗，是彝族民族的历史记载，具有很大的文学价值和历史意义。

“查姆”在彝语中的意思为“大”和“起源”，即万物起源。宏大史诗《查姆》有 120 多“查”。民族文化专家郭思久、陶学良经过广泛搜集，整理出了其中的 11“查”，并对这些原始材料进行整理，出版了汉译版的彝族创世史诗《查姆》。

本书全文翻译彝族史诗《查姆》，分上下部共十个章节，以汉英对照的方式描述了彝族传说中万物的起源，再现了彝族早期对历史的记载。民族民间典籍是少数民族文化传承的重要载体，翻译民族典籍是让世界了解中国民族文化的重要手段，也是将我国的民族文化传播到世界的最有效途径。近几年，在中国文化走向世界步伐加快、中国文化软实力不断提高的大背景下，中国民族民间文化“走出去”的需求日益强烈。借助翻译少数民族典籍能更好地向世界展示我国民族文化的丰富多彩，使世界对我国民族文化的认识更加全面。《查姆》这部民族文学作品英译的完成，将把这部彝族史诗推向世界，有利于我国传统文化的对外传播，让世界各国读者了解认识彝族独特的信仰与文化，并将进一步促进我国南方少数民族民间故事翻译与研究的进一步发展。

本书为汉英对照本，中文版由云南人民出版社 2009 年出版，郭思九、陶学良完成了《查姆》一书的整理与汉译工作，英译文由中南民族大学外国语学院教师杨柳完成。本书的翻译工作得到了中南民族大学外国语学院领导和同事的指导和帮助，在此表示感谢。

由于译者水平有限，理解和表达有不当之处。读者若有发现，敬请批评指正，以便改正。

杨柳

2021 年 7 月

目　录

上　部

下　部

Contents

Volume One

Volume Two

上　　部

Volume One

序诗

人类最早那一代，
他们的名字叫“拉爹”①；
他们只有一只眼，
独眼生在脑门心。

“拉爹”下一代，
名字叫“拉拖”②；
他们有两只直眼睛，
两只直眼朝上生。

“拉拖”的后一代，
名字叫“拉文”③，
他们有两只横眼睛，
两眼平平朝前生。

① 拉爹：独眼睛那代人的名字。

② 拉拖：直眼睛那代人的名字。

③ 拉文：横眼睛那代人的名字。彝族先民把人类分为独眼睛、直眼睛、横眼睛三个时代。

Preface

The first generation of human beings
Was named "La Die①";
They had only one eye,
Which was in the middle of the forehead.

The generation after "La Die"
Was named "La Tuo②";
They had two vertical eyes,
Which pointed straight up.

The generation after "La Tuo"
Was named "La Wen③";
They had two horizontal eyes,
Which pointed forward.

---

① La Die: the name of the one-eyed generation.

② La Tuo: the name of the vertical-eyed generation.

③ La Wen: the name of the horizontal-eyed generation. The Yi ancestors divided human history into three periods: the Era of the One-eyed, the Era of the Vertical-eyed, and the Era of the Horizontal-eyed.

"拉文"是我们的祖先，
最早的"拉文"是两兄妹，
他俩名叫阿朴独姆，
阿朴独姆西①是他们的子孙。

亲亲的阿哥，
亲亲的阿姐，
请慢慢听彝家的"查"②，
请细细听彝家的古根。

① 阿朴独姆西：阿朴独姆是两兄妹的共同名字。阿朴独姆西，意为阿朴独姆的子孙。

② 查：起源。

"La Wen" were our ancestors,
And the earliest "La Wen" were a brother and a sister.
Their name was Apu Dumu,
And Apu Dumuxi① means their offsprings.

Dear brothers,
Dear sisters,
Please listen patiently to Yi people's "Cha"②, and
Please listen carefully to Yi people's Origin.

① Apu Dumuxi: Apu Dumu was the name of both the brother and the sister. Apu Dumuxi means the offspring of Apu Dumu.

② Cha: the origin.

第一章　天地的起源

远古的时候，
天地连成一片。
下面没有地，
上面没有天；
分不出黑夜，
分不出白天。

只有雾露一团团，
只有雾露滚滚翻。
雾露里有地，
雾露里有天；
时昏时暗多变幻，
时清时浊年复年。

天翻成地，
地翻成天，
天地混沌分不清，
天地雾露难分辨。
空中不见飞禽，
地上不见人烟；

Chapter One　The Origin of the Heavens and the Earth

A very long time ago,
The sky and the earth were together as one.
There was no earth below,
Nor was there sky above;
No night was distinguishable, and
No day was distinguishable.

Only clouds of mist circled around, and
Only clouds of mist rolled over and over.
In the clouds of mist was the earth, and
In the clouds of mist was the sky;
Dim and dusky, the clouds were volatile,
Now clear now turbid, year in and year out.

The sky turned into the earth.
The earth turned into the sky.
In the chaos, the two were indistinguishable,
Nor were the two from the clouds of mist.
Birds were not seen in the sky,
Nor were humans seen on the earth.

没有草木生长，
没有座座青山；
没有滔滔大海，
没有滚滚河川；
没有太阳照耀，
没有星斗满天；
没有月亮发光，
更没打雷扯闪。

涅侬倮佐颇，
是所有神仙之王。
他召集众人神仙：
仙王入黄炸当地，
水王罗塔纪，
龙王罗阿玛①，
天王和地王
还有他们的儿女。
众人神聚一起，
共同来商议；
要安排日月星辰，
要铸就宇宙山川，
要造天造地。

① 罗阿玛：全名叫涅侬阿玛，是众龙王之王。

There existed no lush vegetation,
No green mountains,
No roaring seas,
No surging rivers,
No shining sun,
No twinkling stars in the sky,
No glowing moon,
No striking lightning or crashing thunder.

Nienong Luozuopo
Was the head of all immortals.
He summoned all them:
Immortal King—Ruhuang Zhadangdi,
Water Queen—Luo Taji,
Dragon Queen—Luo Ama①
King of Heaven and Earth,
And their children.
Immortals gathered together
To confer with each other.
They were to arrange the sun, the moon and the stars,
Forge the cosmos, mountains and rivers
Create the sky and the earth.

① Luo Ama: full name Nienong Ama, the head of all Dragon Kings.

派龙王罗阿玛，
去到太空中，
种活一棵娑罗树，
树生四枝杈，
一杈生四叶，
四匹叶上四朵花。
这棵娑罗树，
是树木的祖先。
白天不开花，
夜晚白花鲜。

派撒赛萨若埃①，
到一千重天上，
种棵娑罗树，
树生四枝杈，
一杈生四叶，
四匹叶上四朵花。
花开红嫣嫣，
万颗金针刺双眼。
树花白天开，
日日花开照人间。

白天、黑夜两朵花，
轮流开在太空间。
白天开花是太阳，
夜晚开花是月亮；
太阳开花月不明，

① 撒赛萨若埃：涅侬倮佐颇的长子。

Dragon Queen Luo Ama was sent,
Into the space
To plant a shorea tree,
Which had four branches,
Each with four leaves,
Which had on them four flowers.
This shorea tree
Was the ancestor of all trees.
It blossomed not at daytime, but
At night with fresh white blooms.

Sasai Sanuoai① was sent
To the thousandth heaven,
To plant a shorea tree.
Which had four branches,
Each with four leaves,
Which had on them four flowers.
The flowers, when blooming, were bright red,
Like tens and thousands of golden rays pricking the eyes.
The tree flowers bloomed during the day,
Shining upon the earth every day.

Day and night were two flowers,
Bloomed in turn in the space.
The one that flowered during the day was the sun.
The one that flowered at night was the moon.
The moon would darken when the sun flowered.

---

① Sasai Sanuoai: the eldest son of Nienong Luozuopo.

月亮开花星不闪；
两花轮流开，
两花难相见。
十年花不谢，
万载花鲜艳。

派涅依撒萨歇①，
在太空撒上星辰。
抬头望星星，
数也数不完，
夜晚眨眼睛
星光亮闪闪。

星王曾色锡，
笑在太空中。
打开风水门，
雾露缥缈太空间。
雾露里有地，
雾露里有天；
雾露变气育万物，
万物生长天地间。

只有日月星辰，
还无宇宙山川。
还要造山河，
还要造蓝天。

① 涅依撒萨歇：涅依倮佐颇的次子。

The stars would not shimmer when the moon flowered.
The two flowers took turns to bloom,
Never seeing each other.
Flowers didn't wither for ten years,
And they remained bright and fresh forever.

Nienong Sasaxie① was sent
To sprinkle stars in the sky.
High above in the sky,
There were countless stars,
Blinking and
Twinkling at night.

Star King Zeng Sexi,
Laughing in the space,
Opened the Gate of Fengshui
To the space filled with the clouds of mist.
In the clouds of mist was the earth, and
In the clouds of mist was the sky;
The clouds of mist transformed into air to foster everything,
Which grew between the heavens and the earth.

With only the sun, the moon and the stars,
There were not yet the world, mountains or rivers.
Mountains and rivers were still to be created,
So was the blue sky.

---

① Nienong Sasaxie: the second son of Nienong Luozuopo.

神仙之王涅依倮佐颇，
开口来指点：
地要造成簸箕样，
天要造得篾帽圆。
篾帽、簸箕才合得拢，
篾帽、簸箕合成地和天。

造人之神的女儿涅滨矮①，
设法造河川。
造下洪波万顷的大海，
造下纵横的沟渠河川，
造下湖泊和清泉，
造下绿水和深潭。

水王罗塔纪，
是水中神仙。
她用海水养鱼养虾，
鱼在海底游，
虾在水中翻；
她管绿水有方，
绿水四季长流，
绿水映澈蓝天。
她管水里的万物，
她管龙潭深渊；
她管地上的万物，
她管地上的粮棉。

① 涅滨矮：造人之神儿依得罗娃的女儿。

The head of immortals Nienong Luozuopo
Gave instructions:
The earth should be made like a flat wicker tray,
The sky, round like a bamboo-braid hat.
The hat and the wicker tray would match,
Making the earth and the sky.

Nie Binai①, the daughter of the immortal who would create humans,
Created the lakes and rivers.
She created the turbulent and boundless seas,
Vertical and horizontal gullies and rivers,
Lakes and clear springs,
And green waters and deep pools.

Water Queen Luo Taji,
Was a water immortal.
She raised fishes and shrimps in the seawater,
With fishes swimming at the bottom of the sea,
Shrimps rolling in the water;
She did well managing the green water,
Which flowed all seasons long,
Reflecting the blue sky.
She managed everything in the water,
And the abyss of the Dragon Pool;
She managed everything on the earth, and
Managed the grain and cotton on the ground.

---

① Nie Binai: the daughter of Eryi Deluowa who were to create humans.

龙王罗阿玛心最细，
星星走动能听见。
她到九重天上找种子，
种子长在月中间。
月里那棵娑罗树，
树上良种数不完；
奇花异草由人选，
树木药材任人拣，
树上藏有谷子、苞谷，
树上储存果木麻棉；
还有荞子、洋芋，
还有甘蔗蜜甜……
有种籽才有万物，
有万物才有人烟；
有种籽祖先才能生存，
有粮食人类才能繁衍。
罗阿玛呵，想得周到，
罗阿玛呵，想得最远。

涅侬倮佐颇，
开口又指点：
大地造成了平原，
大地并不美观。
地面要有盆地，
地面要有高山；
既要有雨露滋润，
又要有阳光送暖；
这样才能种粮食，
人类才能生存发展。

Dragon Queen Luo Ama was the most meticulous,
Being able to hear the stars walking.
She sought and found seeds from the ninth heaven
And planted it in the middle of the moon.
That shorea tree in the moon
Bore numerous good seeds.
Exotic flowers and unusual plants were for all to choose,
So were trees and herbs.
There were millets and corn on the tree
And fruit, flax and cotton, too,
As well as buckwheat and potatoes.
And sugarcane that was honey sweet…
There had to be seeds first and then myriads of things,
And then humans;
With seeds ancestors could survive, and
With food humans could reproduce.
Ah, Luo Ama, how thoughtful,
Ah, Luo Ama, what a visionary.

Nienong Luozuopo,
Gave orders again:
The earth is now made into plains
And is not beautiful.
There need to be basins on the ground
And high mountains on the earth;
There must be both the rain and dew
And the sunshine for warmth;
That way the grains can grow,
Humans can survive and develop.

龙王罗阿玛呵，
按照涅侬倮佐颇的吩咐，
又来到广阔的平原。
她撒下倾盆大雨，
冲出沟河山川；
冲成峻岭深箐，
冲出丘陵河滩；
大地冒清泉，
遍地流水潺潺。

日复一日，
年复一年，
天上太阳又不亮，
天上月亮又不明。
神仙之王涅侬倮佐颇，
找来水王罗塔纪，
还有罗塔纪姑娘，
共同来商议。

水王罗塔纪说：
“由于日月不干净，
白天黑夜才分不清。”
神仙之王派罗塔纪姑娘，
飞到九千台天上，
去洗月亮和太阳。

Ah, Dragon Queen Luo Ama,
Following the orders of Nienong Luozuopo,
Returned to the vast plains.
She poured heavy rains,
That carved out the rivers and mountains,
Steep cliffs and deep valleys,
Hills and benchlands;
Clear water sprang from under the earth,
Flowing all over the earth.

Day by day,
Year after year,
The sun in the sky was not bright,
Nor was the moon in the sky.
The head of immortals, Nienong Luozuopo,
Asked the Water Queen Luo Taji,
And her daughter Miss Luo Taji,
To come and discuss the matter.

Water Queen Luo Taji said:
"It is because the sun and the moon are not clean,
That it is hard to tell day from night."
The head of immortals sent Miss Luo Taji
To fly up to the nine thousandth heaven
And clean the moon and the sun.

罗塔纪姑娘，
去到撑天的三座山上，
挑来一挑蓝海水，
挑来一挑金海水，
挑来一挑绿海水，
去洗日月身上的灰尘。

罗塔纪姑娘，
洗完星星洗月亮，
洗罢月亮洗太阳。
星星洗得亮晶晶，
星星黑夜眨眼睛；
月亮洗得亮堂堂，
太阳洗得白生生，
太阳白天耀眼明。

罗塔纪姑娘，
洗干净了星星，
洗干净了月亮，
洗干净了太阳。
从此天地不混沌，
昼夜辨得清，
四季分得明。
瞧着日出日落，
就能分出早晚；
看着月出月落
就能分出昼夜；
看着草木盛衰，

Miss Luo Taji,
Went up to the three mountains that held up the sky,
Carrying first the water from the Blue Sea,
Then the water from the Golden Sea,
Then the water from the Green Sea,
To wash off the dust on the sun and the moon.

Miss Luo Taji
Washed the stars and then the moon,
Washed the moon and then the sun.
The stars were washed twinkling-bright,
Blinking their eyes in the dark night.
The moon was washed glowing-bright
And the sun was washed dazzling-bright,
Dazzling the eyes during the day.

Miss Luo Taji,
Washed clean the stars,
Washed clean the moon and
Washed clean the sun.
Ever since then, the sky and the earth are separated,
With distinctive day and night,
And four clear seasons.
By looking at the rising and the setting sun,
One can tell morning and dusk;
By looking at the rising and the setting moon,
One can distinguish day and night;
By looking at the change of vegetation,

能知寒暑冷暖；
瞧着庄稼生长，
能分四季变幻。

日月怎样走动？
白天黑夜怎样循环？
白天太阳走，
夜晚月亮转；
还有满天星星，
跟着月亮眨眼。

太阳和月亮，
轮流转玉盘。
它们是天地的眼睛，
专给大地照明送温暖。
天一睁眼，
太阳就露笑脸；
天一闭眼，
月亮、星星笑做一团。

天地间的事，
地动是第一。
地转到金海旁边，
太阳出来啦！
地转到蓝海旁边，
月亮出来啦！
地转到绿海旁边，
星星出来啦！

One can know the change of weather;
By looking at the crops growing,
One can follow the cycle of the four seasons.

How did the sun and the moon move?
How did the day and the night follow each other?
During the day the sun moved
And at night the moon did;
There were also the stars all over the sky,
Blinking with the moon.

The sun and the moon,
Turned the jade plate in turn.
They were the eyes of the sky and the earth,
Dedicated to lighting and warming the earth.
When the sky opened its eyes,
The sun was smiling.
When the sky closed its eyes,
The moon and the stars laughed together.

Between the heaven and the earth,
The motion of the earth was the first.
When the earth moved close to the Golden Sea,
The sun came out!
When the earth moved close to the Blue Sea,
The moon came out!
When the earth moved close to the Green Sea,
The stars came out!

万物在动中生，
万物在动中演变。
不动嘛不生，
不生嘛不长，
这就是天地的起始，
这就是万物的来源。

彝家把这个时代，
叫做托得多查①，
汉家把这个时代，
叫做盘古分天地。

① 托得多查：音译，查，源也；托得多，天地的意思；托得多查，天地的起源。

Everything was born in motion
And evolved in it, too.
Nothing can live without motion,
Or can grow without life.
This was the beginning of the heavens and the earth,
The origin of all things.

The Yi people named this era,
Tuo Deduo Cha①.
And the Han people named this era,
Pangu Separating the Heavens and the Earth.

---

① Tuo Deduo Cha: transliteration. Cha: origin. Tuo Deduo: the heavens and the earth. Tuo Deduo Cha: the origin of the Heavens and the Earth.

第二章　独眼睛时代

有了日月星辰，
有了宇宙山川，
不能没有人烟；
有了江河湖泊，
有了种子粮棉，
不能没有人生活在天地间。

雾露缥缈大地，
变成绿水一潭。
水中有个姑娘，
名叫赛依列①，
她说“要造独眼睛时代的人”，
就叫儿依得罗娃最先来造人。
儿依得罗娃，

① 赛依列：龙王的姑娘。

Chapter Two　The Era of the One-eyed

With the moon and the stars,
With the universe, mountains and rivers,
There must be humans;
With rivers and lakes,
With seeds, grains and cotton,
There must be humans living between the sky and the earth.

The clouds of mist that lingered on the earth,
Turned into a pool of green water.
In the water was a girl,
Whose name was Sai Yilie①.
She said, "We must create humans of the One-eyed Era."
She asked Eryi Deluowa as the first one to make humans.
Eryi Deluowa,

① Sai Yilie: daughter of Dragon Queen.

造出人类的第一代祖先①，
他们的名字叫“拉爹”。
他们是天地的儿女，
他们是太阳的儿女，
他们是月亮的儿女，
他们是星星的儿女
这代人只有一只眼，
独只眼睛长在哪里？
独只眼生在脑门心。

独眼睛这代人，
不会说话，
不会种田，
像野兽一样过光阴。
今天跟老虎打架，
明天和豹子硬拼；
人吃野兽，
野兽也吃人。
常常互相争斗，
有时还会人吃人。

① 儿依得罗娃造人之说，原传说中还有两种说法：一种是她“塑起了两个人，男的那个眼睛有八只，耳朵有九只；女的那个手有四只，脚有两只……他们的眼睛不眨”。另一种说法，她“塑了两个人，男人塑了八只眼，八只眼睛看万山；耳朵塑了九只，九只耳朵听得远；还塑了一只特殊眼，眼睛不眨看得宽。女人捏了六只手，六只巧手能胜天；女人捏成六只脚，六脚走得快”。这些传说有一定的参考价值，特注录于此。

Created the first generation of the human ancestors①,
Whose name was "La Die".
They were children of the heavens and the earth,
Children of the sun,
Children of the moon,
Children of the stars.
People of this generation had only one eye.
Where was the single eye?
It was in middle of the forehead.

This one-eyed generation
Could neither speak
Nor farm,
Passing the time like the beasts did.
One day they fought with the tigers and
Another day they fought with the leopards.
They ate the beasts while
The beasts ate them, too.
They fought like this constantly
Sometimes eating their own kind.

---

① There are two versions of the legend of Eryi Deluowa creating human beings. One is that she "created two persons. The male had eight eyes and nine ears. The female had four hands and two feet... Their eyes did not blink". The other version is that she "created two persons. The male had eight eyes which could see as far as tens and thousands of mountains away; nine ears which could hear from just as far away; a special eye that never blinked and had a wide vision. The female had six hands with extraordinary dexterity and six feet with great speed". These versions could be helpful and therefore are noted here.

独眼睛这代人，
深山老林作房屋，
野岭岩洞常栖身。
石头作工具，
木棒当武器，
在风雨雷电中穿行。

独眼睛这代人，
树叶做衣裳，
乱草当被盖，
渴了喝凉水，
饿了吃野果，
草根树皮来充饥。
他们不知酸甜味，
他们苦辣不能分。

独眼睛这代人啊，
困了树下睡，
病了树下哼。
高兴拉着树枝跳，
有时狂叫有时笑，
在哭笑中生存。

独眼睛这代人啊，
慢慢认识野兽习性：
力大不过野猪，
凶猛不过老虎，

This one-eyed generation
Used the mountains and forests as their houses,
Hills and caves as their shelters.
With stones as their tools and
Wooden sticks as their weapons,
They moved back and forth through the wind, the rain, the thundering and the lightning.

This one-eyed generation
Made clothes out of tree leaves,
Quilts out of grass.
They drank cold water to quench their thirst,
Ate wild berries to quell their hunger,
And survived on the grass roots and tree barks.
They could not tell the sweet from the sour,
Nor the bitter from the spicy.

This one-eyed generation,
Slept under the trees when sleepy,
Groaned under the trees when sick.
They dragged along tree twigs and jumped when happy,
Sometimes howling and sometimes laughing,
Lived in the midst of crying and laughing.

This one-eyed generation
Gradually came to know the habits of the beasts:
Wild boars were the strongest,
Tigers were the most fierce,

胆小不过麂子，
善良不过马鹿，
能爬树的是猴子，
没肝胆的是蚂蚁……

青松和果松一起生，
野鸡和鸟雀一起生，
青蛙和石蚌一起生，
家畜和野兽一起生，
人和猴子一起生，
人和野兽混在一起。

独眼睛这代人啊，
猴子和人分不清。
猴子生儿子，
也是独眼睛。
猴子摘野果，
丢给猴儿吃；
猴儿拾野果，
仔细看形状，
猴儿嚼野果，
尝出果子的滋味。

独眼小猴儿，
主意又多心又灵。
拔来了秧草，
在果树上结疙瘩；
果树的名字，

Muntjacs were the most timid,
Red deer were the kindest.
Monkeys were tree climbers,
And ants had no livers or gallbladders...

The green pines and Korean pines stood together.
Pheasants and wildfowls lived together.
Frogs and Rana spinosa stayed together.
Livestock and wild beasts resided together.
Humans and monkeys grew together.
Humans and wild beasts coexisted.

The one-eyed generation,
The monkeys and humans were alike.
The monkeys' children
Were also one-eyed.
Monkeys picked wild berries
To feed their young;
The little moneys picked up the wild berries and
Looked closely at the shape.
They chewed on the wild berries and
Tasted the flavor of the fruits.

The one-eyed little monkeys
Had lots of ideas and quick minds.
They pulled the rice seedlings
And tied knots to the fruit trees.
The names of the fruit trees

用疙瘩来区分；
疙瘩结在树上，
树果慢慢分得清。

独眼睛这代人啊，
没有找到火种，
冷热不知道，
生熟两不分。
他们熬过严寒和酷暑，
他们度过数不清的冬春；
冷水拦野果，
食物尽生吞。

不知过了多少代，
独眼睛这代人，
用石头敲硬果，
溅起火星星。
火星落在树叶上，
野火烧起山林。
果子滚进火堆里，
熟果味更醇。

聪明的独眼人，
把火的好处记在心。
用火来御寒冷，
用火来作伴侣，
用火来烧东西……
生吃树果有生味，

Were distinguished by the number of knots.
With the knots tied on the trees,
They learned gradually the kinds of tree fruits.

The one-eyed generation,
Having not discovered tinder,
Did not know the difference between the cold and the hot,
The raw and the cooked.
They survived the harsh cold and intense heat,
And countless winters and springs.
They ate wild fruits with cold water
And ate everything raw.

No one knows how many years had passed,
When the one-eyed generation
Struck the nuts with the stone
With sparks flying off.
The sparks fell on the leaves,
Starting the wildfire in the forests.
The berries rolled into the fire,
And the burnt fruits were more tasty.

Smart one-eyed people
Remembered the benefits of the fire.
They used it to shield themselves from the cold,
To be their companion, and
To cook things...
Raw fruits tasted raw,

熟吃树果味更美。
从此冷暖能分辨，
从此生熟能分辨。

独眼睛这代人，
茹苦含辛，
不知道种粮食，
人类难生存。

神仙之王涅侬倮佐颇，
仙王入黄炸当地，
龙王罗阿玛，
水王罗塔纪，
一齐来商量，
共同出主意：
“龙要放出来，
雨要落下地；
粮食种子要撒下，
人才有吃的东西。”

水王罗塔纪，
打开四海门，
放出四海水。
龙王罗阿玛，
四方行风雨。

东方放绿龙，
南方放红龙，

And cooked fruits were more delicious.
From then on they could tell the cold from the warm,
Could distinguish the raw from the cooked.

The one-eyed generation
Endured much hardships and hard labor.
But without knowing how to farm,
The human race had a difficult time to survive.

The head of immortals Nienong Luozuopo,
Immortal King Ruhuang Zhadangdi,
Dragon Queen Luo Ama,
Water Queen Luo Taji,
Talked with each other and
Together came up with an idea:
"The dragon must be released
To let the rain fall.
The seeds of crops must be sown,
So that people have food to eat."

Water Queen Luo Taji
Opened the gates of the four seas,
Released the four seas' waters.
Dragon Queen Luo Ama,
Cast wind and rain in four directions.

The green dragon was sent out to the east,
The red dragon to the south,

西方放白龙，
北方放黑龙。
四方刮风，
四方播雨。

仙王入黄炸当地，
四方去撒种。
粮食种子丢一把，
粮种遍地长，
人间处处有食粮。
树木种子撒一筐，
树木遍山冈，
彝家山寨树木密，
是因种树撒得多。

龙王罗阿玛，
舀起四瓢水：
东方浇瓢绿龙水，
刮风又下雨，
种子冒嫩芽，
草木叶新蕊。
雨下到的地方，
庄稼都抽穗。

南方浇瓢红龙水，
刮风又下雨，
百花竞开松柏翠；
有雨的地方，
桑麻甘蔗节节生。

The white dragon to the west,
The black dragon to the north.
The wind blew in four directions.
The rain came down in four directions.

Immortal King Ruhuang Zhadangdi,
Sowed in four directions.
One handful grain seeds were scattered
That grew all over the earth and
Fed people everywhere on the earth.
A basketful tree seeds were cast over the mountains
That grew trees everywhere on the mountains.
The trees in the Yi villages were thick
Because so many tree seeds had been cast.

Dragon Queen Luo Ama,
Scooped up water four times.
One scoop of the green dragon water was for the east,
So that with the wind and the rain,
The seeds sprouted.
Vegetation bore stamens.
Where the rain fell,
Crops grew ears of grain.

One scoop of the red dragon water was for the south,
So that with the wind and the rain,
Countless flowers bloomed and cedars turned green;
Where there was rain,
Mulberries, flax and sugar cane grew taller and taller.

西方浇瓢白龙水，
刮风又下雨，
雾露全散尽，
种子落土里。
风吹到的地方，
蜂飞蝶舞百鸟啼；
雨落到的地方，
土地湿润冒清水。

北方浇瓢黑龙水，
刮风又下雨，
草木常开花，
枯树发新枝；
风吹到的地方，
桃李含苞开鲜花；
雨下到的地方，
枝头果实累累。

四方浇了四瓢水，
四季有风又有雨，
山山流出清泉水，
五谷种得成。

独眼睛时代，
世上万物样样有：
一颗米有鸡蛋大，
谷子长得像竹林；
一粒苞谷鸭蛋大，

One scoop of the white dragon water was for the west,
So that with the wind and the rain,
The clouds of mist cleared away
And the seeds fell into the earth.
Where the wind blew,
Bees flew, butterflies danced and birds sang;
Where the rain fell,
The land was moist and clear water emerged.

One scoop of the black dragon water was for the north,
So that with the wind and the rain,
Vegetation often flowered,
And dead trees grew new branches;
Where the wind blew,
Peach trees and plum trees budded and flowered;
Where the rain fell,
The branches were full of fruits.

Four scoops of water for the four directions,
The wind and the rain for the four seasons,
Spring water flowed out of every mountain,
So all kinds of grains could grow.

During the One-eyed Era,
The world had everything:
A grain of rice was as big as an egg.
Millets grew like the bamboo forest.
A corn kernel was as big as a duck egg.

苞谷秆子高过房顶；
一颗蚕豆鹅蛋大，
蚕豆苗棵高过人。

独眼睛这代人，
不分男和女，
不分长幼尊卑；
不分白天黑夜
不分月大月小，
不分秋夏冬春。
怪事天天有，
灾难月月生。
马乱踢人，
牛乱顶人，
鸡乱啄人，
到处乱纷纷。

仙王入黄炸当地，
手摇娑罗枝，
风雨当马骑。
来到泽梗子①，
来到黑夺方②。
找来独眼人，

① 泽梗子：地名。
② 黑夺方：地名。

The corn stalk grew taller than the roof.
A broad bean was as big as a goose egg.
The broad bean seedlings were taller than a person.

The one-eyed generation
Did not differentiate men and women,
The young and the old,
The noble and the humble,
Day and night,
Long month and short month.
Or autumn, summer, winter and spring.
Strange things happened every day;
Disasters happened every month.
Horses kicked people.
Bulls gored people.
Chickens pecked people.
Chaos was everywhere.

Immortal King Ruhuang Zhadangdi,
Waving a shorea tree branch,
Rode the windy rain as a horse.
He came to Ze Gengzi①
And Hei Duofang②.
He found an one-eyed person

---

① Ze Gengzi: name of a place.
② Hei Duofang: name of a place.

吩咐他管理这代人：
“你管三千九百年，
一年四季要分明。
年头月尾要分清，
撒种收割要分清，
世上的人归你管，
你把道理说给众人听。”

独眼睛这代人，
辜负了仙王一片心。
他不过问昼夜，
年月他不分；
太阳月亮他不看，
四季分不清；
播种收割他不管，
庄稼杂草遍地生。

独眼睛这代人，
道理也不讲，
长幼也不分；
儿子不养爹妈，
爹妈不管儿孙。
饿了就互相撕吃，
吵嘴又打架，
时时起纠纷。

And ask him to manage this generation:
"You will be in charge for 3, 900 years,
With clearly observed four seasons.
Be clear about the beginning of the year and the end of the month,
The sowing and harvesting seasons.
You are in charge of the people of the world,
So explain to help them understand."

This one-eyed generation,
Let the Immortal King down.
That person paid no attention to day and night,
Could not tell year from month.
He did not look at the sun or the moon,
Or tell the four seasons.
He didn't care about sowing or harvesting,
Let the weeds grew everywhere with the crops.

The one-eyed generation,
Was unreasonable.
They did not differentiate the elderly and the young;
Sons did not support their parents,
Who did not raise their children or grandchildren.
Hungry, they ate each other,
Bickering and squabbling,
Quarrelling and fighting all the time.

神仙之王涅依倮佐颇，
仙王入黄炸当地，
龙王罗阿玛，
水王罗塔纪，
一齐来商量，
共同出主意：
“独眼睛这代人心不好，
要换掉这代人。
要找好心人，
重新繁衍子孙。”

入黄炸当地，
驾着风雨乘着云，
来到泽梗子，
来到黑夺方；
他扮作“讨饭人”，
沿村去乞讨，
查访好心人。

“讨饭人”见人就下跪，
磕头又作揖：
“好心的人啊，
我肚子又饿口又渴，
给点东西填肚子，
给点东西润嘴唇！”

The head of all immortals, Nienong Luozuopo,
Immortal King Ruhuang Zhadangdi,
Dragon Queen Luo Ama,
Water Queen Luo Taji,
Came together,
And came up with an idea:
"The one-eyed generation is not kind-hearted
And should be replaced.
Find the kind-hearted
To reproduce offspring."

Ruhuang Zhadangdi,
Riding the windy rain and the clouds,
Came to Ze Gengzi
And Hei Duofang.
Pretending to be a "beggar",
He begged for food around the village
To search for a kind-hearted person.

The "beggar" knelt to everyone he met,
Kowtowing and saluting:
"Kind-hearted people,
I am hungry and thirsty.
Please give me something to fill my stomach
And something to moisten my lips!"

独眼睛人呀，
不给他饭，
不给他水，
张嘴就骂他，
伸手就打他，
出脚就踢他，
把“讨饭人”撵出门。

“讨饭人”又走了一家，
磕头又作揖：
“好心的兄弟呀，
我肚子又饿口又渴，
给点东西填肚子，
给点冷水润润唇!”

那一家人呀，
不给他饭，
不给他水，
不给东西还乱骂，
拳打脚踢推出门。

“讨饭人”走到大路旁，
遇上一个做活人。
他做活没有牛，
木棒来耕耘，
累得满面汗淋淋。
“讨饭人”走上前，
叩头又作揖：

The one-eyed people
Gave him neither food
Nor water.
They opened their mouths only to curse him,
Reached out their hands only to hit him,
Lifted their feet only to kick him,
Driving the "beggar" out of their doors.

The "beggar" went to another family,
Kowtowing and saluting:
"Kind-hearted brothers,
I am hungry and thirsty.
Please give me something to fill my stomach
And some cold water to moisten my lips!"

That family,
Gave him neither food
Nor water.
They gave him nothing but cursing,
Punching, kicking, and pushing him out of the door.

The "beggar" came by the road
And saw a man working by himself.
He farmed without cattle and
Plowed with a stick,
Tired and sweaty.
The "beggar" went up to him,
Kowtowing and saluting:

"好心的阿哥呀，
我肚饿口又渴，
给点东西填肚子，
给点冷水润润唇！"

做活人扶起"讨饭人"：
"出门的阿哥啊，
天上鹰顾鹰，
地上苦人帮苦人。
饿了同我吃野果，
渴了和我喝凉水。
野果当饭味道甜，
凉水解渴爽透心。"

"讨饭人"忙道谢，
"我不吃你的野果，
我不喝你的凉水，
世上所有的人，
数你最讲理；
世上所有的人，
数你最有良心。"

"我把实话告诉你：
在这块天下，
在这块地上，
独眼睛这代人要不得，
要换掉这代人；
干旱要降临，
万物晒死活不成。"

"Kind-hearted brother,
I am hungry and thirsty.
Please give me something to fill my stomach,
And some cold water to moisten my lips!"

The working man helped get the "beggar" on his feet:
"Dear brother who is far away from home,
Hawks look after hawks in the sky,
And the poor help the poor on the earth.
Eat wild berries with me when hungry,
And drink cold water with me when thirsty.
Wild berries are sweet meals for us to have,
And cold water quenches thirst and makes us cool."

The "beggar" quickly thanked him,
"I won't eat your wild berries
Or drink your cold water,
Of all people in the world,
You are the most understanding;
Of all people in the world,
You are the most kind-hearted."

"Let me tell you the truth:
Under this sky,
On this earth,
The one-eyed generation must go,
Must be replaced;
A great drought will come
To kill all things."

做活人忙询问：
“世上遭干旱，
世上人要绝，
到底咋个整？
请您来指引！”

“讨饭人”笑盈盈：
“阿哥莫忧虑，
阿哥莫担心，
我把葫芦送给你。
葫芦里有喝不完的水，
葫芦里有吃不尽的粮，
还有长生不老药。
你一天喝一口水，
你一天吃一把米。
灾难来了你进葫芦去，
三年不会缺水，
三年不会饿肚子。”

“讨饭人”解下葫芦，
做活人接过宝贝，
只听一阵风声起，
不见了“讨饭人”的踪影。

The working man asked hurriedly:
"If the earth will suffer a drought
And lose all its people,
What can I do?
Please guide me!"

The "beggar" smiled:
"Not to worry, brother,
Not to be troubled.
Here is a gourd that I will give you.
The gourd has water that can never be drunk up,
Grains that can never be eaten up,
And elixirs that can make one immortal.
Take a sip of water a day,
A handful of rice a day.
Get into the gourd when the disaster comes,
With no shortage of water for three years,
No hunger for three years."

The "beggar" untied the gourd from himself,
And the working man accepted it.
With the sound of a gust of wind,
The "beggar" vanished.

第三章 直眼睛时代

一、干旱来临

天上水门关了，
四方水门关了。
三年见不到闪电，
三年听不到雷声，
三年不刮一阵清风，
三年不洒一滴甘霖。

大地晒干了，
草木渐渐凋零；
大地晒裂了，
地上烟尘滚滚；
大海晒涸了，
鱼虾化成泥；
江河晒干了，
沙石碎成灰；

Chapter Three The Era of the Vertical-eyed

I. The Drought Was Coming

The water gates in the sky were closed.
The water gates of all the four directions were closed.
There was no lightning to be seen for three years,
No thundering to be heard for three years,
No breeze to blow for three years, and
Not a drop of rain to fall in three years.

The earth was dried up,
With all vegetation gradually withering away.
The ground cracked,
With smoke of dust rolling everywhere.
The seas dried up,
With fishes and shrimps burnt into mud.
The rivers and lakes dried up,
With sand and stone crushed into ashes.

老虎豹子晒死，
马鹿岩羊晒绝，
不见雀鸟展翅，
不见蛇蝎爬行；
飞禽走兽绝迹，
大地荒凉天昏沉。

顶天柱被晒断，
三座大山被晒塌，
星星晒得出汗，
月亮晒出泪水，
娑罗树晒得枯黄。

众神之王涅侬倮佐颇，
仙王入黄炸当地，
龙王罗阿玛，
水王罗塔纪，
还有罗塔纪的姑娘，
一齐为商量，
共同出主意：
“天旱三年，
江河干涸，
大地开裂，
草木枯萎，
玉石俱焚，
独眼人晒死。
要留‘做活人’，
作大地的主人。”

Tigers and leopards were burned to death.
Red deer and blue sheep were extinct.
No birds could be seen.
No snakes or scorpions were crawling.
All birds and beasts disappeared.
The earth was desolate and drowsy.

The pole holding the sky was dried up and broken.
The three mountains were dried up and crumbled.
The stars sweated by the sunshine.
The moon shed tears by the sunshine,
The shorea trees shrivelled and yellowed.

The head of all immortals, Nienong Luozuopo,
Immortal King Ruhuang Zhadangdi,
Dragon Queen Luo Ama,
Water Queen Luo Taji,
And the daughter of Luo Taji,
Met and
Came up with an idea:
"During the three years of drought,
The rivers and lakes dried up;
The ground cracked open;
The vegetation withered;
The jades and rocks turned into ashes;
And the one-eyed generation was burnt to death.
The 'working man' was preserved
To be the master of the earth."

入黄炸当地，
驾着风雨乘着云，
寻找好心人；
东边西边找，
南边北边寻，
不见那个做活人。

仙王来到泽梗子，
仙王来到黑夺方，
四方巡察遍，
不见一个人影。
仿佛有雀鸟在飞，
好像有什么在唱？
仙王仔细瞧，
只见蜜蜂扇翅膀；
仙王仔细听，
听到蜜蜂嗡嗡唱。
仙王开口问：
“小蜜蜂啊小蜜蜂，
你飞西又飞东，
你略遇见做活人？”

蜜蜂嗡嗡把话讲：
“苏罗赛文地方，
赛措山头上，
有两棵香樟树，
树上有一对猴子，

Immortal King Ruhuang Zhadangdi,
Riding the windy rain and the clouds,
Looked for that kind-hearted person.
He looked from east to west,
From south to north,
But could not find that working man.

The Immortal King came to Ze Gengzi
And Hei Duofang.
He inspected all the four directions,
But did not see anyone.
It looked as if a bird was flying,
Or someone was singing?
The Immortal King looked carefully
And saw a bee fanning the wings;
The Immortal King listened carefully
And heard the bees buzzing.
The Immortal King asked:
"Little bee, little bee,
Flying west and east,
Have you seen a working man?"

The bee buzzed:
"In Suluosaiwen,
On the top of Hill Saicuo,
There are two camphor trees.
On the tree are a pair of monkeys

树上有斑鸠一双，
树下有两个石头，
石头旁边有两蓬青草，
青草旁边有一对牛羊，
牛羊旁边有猪狗一对。
大树下，石头上，
不见做活人，
倒是坐着一个独眼郎。
他一无弟妹，
二无父母，
三无兄长，
独自一人甚凄凉。

“这个独眼人嘛，
烈日没有把他晒伤；
他时而烦闷，
他时而歌唱。
他撒尿在树下，
枯树披绿装；
尿滴在石头上，
石头长出青苔；
尿水落在青草上，
青草嫩汪汪；
牛羊吃了青草，
牛羊更肥壮；
猪狗吃了青草，
猪狗免病伤；
猴子吃了树果，

And a couple of turtledoves.
Under the tree are two rocks,
Standing by which are two clumps of green grass,
By which are cattle and sheep,
By which are a pig and a dog.
Under the big tree and on the rocks,
I do not see any man working,
Yet there is a one-eyed man.
He has no younger siblings,
or parents,
or older brothers,
Alone and sad.

"This one-eyed person
Was not hurt by the burning sun;
He is bored sometimes
And sings other times.
When he pees under the tree
The withered tree turns green.
When the pee drops on the rocks,
The rocks grow moss.
When the pee falls on the grass,
The grass turns tender green.
When the cattle and sheep eat the green grass
They grow fatter and stronger.
When the pig and dog eat the grass,
They are free of illnesses or injuries.
When the monkeys eat the fruits from the tree,

猴子林中最欢畅；
斑鸠吃了果子，
斑鸠能展翅飞翔；
蜜蜂采了树花，
蜜蜂先把蜜糖尝。”

仙王听了蜜蜂的话，
很快来到苏罗赛文地方，
很快来到赛措山头上。
他在两棵树下，
果然寻到独眼郎。

独眼人见了仙王，
磕头又作揖，
热泪滚滚话儿长：
“神仙呵，救命的恩人！
万里路上不见人，
伴我的只有太阳；
千里路上不见树，
只剩两棵香樟；
百里路上无飞鸟，
只有斑鸠低声唱；
树上不见虫鸣，
只有蜜蜂采花忙；
十里路上不见走兽，

The monkeys are the most cheerful in the forest.
When the turtledoves eat the fruits,
The turtledoves can spread the wings and fly.
When the bees gather honey from the tree flowers,
The bees themselves taste the honey first."

The Immortal King listened to the bee
And soon came to Suluosaiwen
And then to the top of Hill Saicuo.
Under the two trees,
He indeed found the one-eyed man.

Seeing the Immortal King,
The one-eyed person kowtowed and saluted.
With tears rolling down, he said:
"Immortal, my life-saving benefactor!
I do not see anyone on the road for tens and thousands of li①
Except for the sun to be my companion;
I do not see any tree on the road for thousands of li
Except for the two camphor trees;
There are no birds on the road for hundreds of li
Except for the cooing turtledoves;
There are no insects chirping in the trees
Except for the bees busy gathering honey from the flowers;
There are no beasts on the road for tens of li

① li: a unit of length equal to 500 meters.

只有猪狗一对，
只有牛羊一双；
五里路上找不到粮和水，
只有葫芦里的一点水和粮。
我对着大地呼救，
回答我的只有风声簌簌响。
究竟谁能把晒焦的大地变样？
究竟谁能和我做伴成双？

“独水难流淌，
独鸟难飞翔，
独木不成林
独花难飘香，
独个巴掌拍不响，
独人难抗旱魔和灾荒。
恩人呵，神仙！
你能腾云驾雾，
求求你设法解旱荒！”

仙王开口把话讲：
“好心人啊不用慌，
十天之内有人来，
知心朋友会帮忙，
有人伴你会成双。”
说罢驾着清风腾空去，
飞回缥缈太空中。

Except for a pig and a dog,
And cattle and sheep;
There is no food or water on the road for five li.
Except for the bit of water and food in the gourd.
I call on the earth for help
But receive only the wind blowing.
Who can change the charred land?
Who can be my companion?

"It's hard for a drop of water to flow.
It is difficult for a single bird to fly.
One tree cannot make a forest.
One flower cannot spread fragrance far.
One hand cannot clap.
One person can hardly fight the drought and famine.
My benefactor, the immortal!
You can ride the cloud and the fog.
Please help to end the drought!"

The Immortal King opened his mouth and said:
"Kind-hearted person, do not be afraid.
Someone will come within ten days,
Someone who understands you will help you,
Someone who will be your companion."
Having said that, the Immortal King mounted the breeze,
Flying back into the misty space.

仙王派出姑娘撒赛歇，
来到苏罗赛文地方，
来到赛措山上，
来到独眼人身旁。

独眼人一见仙姑娘，
愁容变笑脸，
忙把客人迎进房：
“亲亲的阿姐呀，
我这里没有板凳，
请坐树叶上；
我这里没有水喝，
只有葫芦水；
我这里没有粮食，
请把野果尝一尝。”

仙姑娘说：
“不喝你的葫芦水，
不吃你的救命粮。”
她把独眼人细打量：
独眼人头发白得像棉花，
头上还有瓦雀窝；
全身黑得像栎炭，
身上有麂子，
脸像干树叶一样黄；
眉毛长得像茅草蓬，
眉毛丛中有野蜂；
手指像竹节，

The Immortal King sent his daughter Sa Saixie
To Suluosaiwen,
To Hill Saicuo,
To the side of the one-eyed person.

As soon as the one-eyed person saw the fairy,
His sad face turned into smile,
And he welcomed the guest into the room:
"My dear sister,
I don't have a bench here,
So please sit on the tree leaves;
I don't have drinking water here,
Only the water in the gourd;
I have no food here,
So please try the wild berries."

The fairy said:
"I won't drink your gourd water,
Nor eat your life-saving food."
She looked at the one-eyed person carefully:
He had hair white like cotton,
Where there was also a nest of sparrow;
His whole body was black like charcoal,
With muntjac attached to it.
His face was as yellow as dry leaves.
His eyebrows looked like clumps of thatch,
Where there were wild bees.
His fingers looked like bamboos,

手皮粗得像松树皮；
脚像龙爪子，
脚裂有筷子宽，
脚裂里有麻蛇，
脚板上有石蚌；
穿的是棕树皮，
远看像囤箩。
仙姑娘越看越难看，
乘着雾露飞上了天。

涅侬倮佐颇，
召集众神仙来商量：
“还是请罗塔纪姑娘，
下到地上去帮忙。”

罗塔纪姑娘，
舀了四瓢水，
来到苏罗赛文地方，
来到赛措山上。
她拿根棍子，
指着独眼人头上的瓦雀，
“你去树上做窝。”
指着眉毛上的野蜂，
“你去悬崖上落脚。”
指着肚子上的麂子，
“你去老箐里生活。”
指着脚缝里的麻蛇，
“你到空心树里去住。”

And the skin of his hands was thick like the pine bark.
His feet looked like dragon claws
And the cracks on them were wide as chopsticks,
With snakes in the cracks
And Rana spinosa on the soles of his feet.
He was covered with some palm bark,
Looking like a grain basket from afar.
The more the fairy looked at him the uglier he got.
Riding the dewy fog, she flew into the sky.

Nienong Luozuopo
Summoned the immortals for a consultation:
"Ask Miss Luo Taji
To go down to the earth again to help."

Miss Luo Taji,
With four scoops of water,
Came to Suluosaiwen,
To Hill Saicuo.
She took a stick and
Pointed at the sparrow on the head of the one-eyed person,
"Go and make a nest on the tree";
Pointed at the wild bees on his eyebrows,
"Go and settle on the cliffs";
Pointed at the muntjac on his stomach,
"Go and live in the old bamboo grove";
Pointed at the snakes in the cracks of his feet,
"Go and live in the hollow trees";

指着脚板上的石蚌，
“你到沟塘里唱歌。”

罗塔纪姑娘，
对独眼人讲：
“好心的做活人啊，
你不用焦虑，
我给你带来四瓢水，
你快拿去洗身子。”

独眼人接过四瓢水，
一瓢水洗头发，
白发变黑发；
一瓢水洗手，
粗手变嫩手；
一瓢水洗脚，
脚裂合拢了，
行路似风响；
一瓢水洗身子，
污垢全洗净，
独眼睛变成直眼睛，
鼻子剪刀样，
下巴鸡蛋圆，
嘴唇像鹦哥，
脸上闪红光，
老人变成少年郎。

Pointed at the Rana spinosa on the soles of his feet,
"Hum in the ditches and ponds."

Miss Luo Taji
Said to the one-eyed person:
"Ah, kind-hearted working man,
You don't have to worry.
I brought you four scoops of water.
Go and wash yourself quickly."

The one-eyed person took the four scoops of water:
He used one to wash his hair,
And its color changed from white to black;
He used another one to wash his hands,
And their skin changed from rough to tender;
He used a third one to wash his feet,
And the cracks on his feet healed,
So that he could walk like the wind blowing;
He used the last one to wash his body,
And the dirt was completely gone.
One eye turned into vertical eyes,
His nose like scissors,
His chin round like an egg,
His lips like a parrot's,
His face glowing,
The old man changed into a youngster.

罗塔纪姑娘，
给直眼人打扮梳妆。
给他取下树叶帽，
给他取下树叶裳；
叫他脱去绿叶裤，
全身换新装。
蝴蝶围着他飞，
蜜蜂围着他唱。

直眼睛人呀，
望着罗塔纪姑娘，
两脚跪下地，
两手忙作揖：
“仙姑娘啊仙姑娘，
我用什么感激你？”

罗塔纪姑娘，
只笑不回答，
彩云当马骑，
回到了天上。
她把直眼人的美貌，
告诉仙姑娘撒赛歇。

仙姑撒赛歇，
重返苏罗赛文地方，
重回赛措山上。
她找到了直眼睛人，
看他打扮不一样；

Miss Luo Taji
Dressed up this vertical-eyed person.
Taking off the leaf cap,
The leaf clothes,
And the green leaf pants,
She replaced all with new ones.
The butterflies flew around him,
And the bees sang around him.

The vertical-eyed person
Looked at Miss Luo Taji.
On his knees,
He bowed to her:
"Fairy, fairy,
What can I do to thank you?"

Miss Luo Taji
Smiled but gave no reply.
Riding the clouds as a horse,
She returned to heaven.
She described how handsome the vertical-eyed person was
To Fairy Sa Saixie.

Fairy Sa Saixie,
Returned to Suluosaiwen,
To Hill Saicuo.
She found the vertical-eyed person
And saw that he dressed differently:

肩套黑领褂，
身穿白布衣，
鞋子三道花，
头戴竹篾帽，
一身新衣裳。
他用棍子打树果，
敲下树果做食粮。

仙姑撒赛歇，
高高兴兴开了腔：
“摘果的人呀，
请问是男还是女？
是男嘤略有妻子
是女嘤略有丈夫？”

直眼人忙回答：
“世上只剩我一人，
我是没有妻子的孤苦人！”

“阿哥啊阿哥，
世上只有我一个女人。
我有话儿问问你，
要是答对了，
我俩做夫妻。”

直眼人忙点头，
“先请阿妹唱。”

Under the black cape
Was a white outfit
And shoes with three flowers,
His hat made of bamboo—
All new from head to toe.
He used a stick to knock off fruits
and used them as his food.

Fairy Sa Saixie
Said merrily:
"The fruit-picking person,
Are you a male or a female?
If a male, do you have a wife?
If a female, do you have a husband?"

The vertical-eyed person answered in a hurry:
"Only myself live in the world.
I am a lonely man without a wife!"

"Brother, brother,
I am the only woman in the world.
I have questions for you.
If you can answer correctly,
We can be husband and wife."

The vertical-eyed person nodded eagerly,
"Please sing first, my sister."

“阿哥啊，阿哥！
世上不放盐能吃的是哪样？
地上不撒种能结果的是哪样？
山上不用栽种能捡来吃的是哪样？
不用喂养能吃肉的是哪样？
有嘴不说话的是哪样？
无嘴响四方的是哪样？
知道白天黑夜的是哪样？……”

“阿姐呀，阿姐！
世上不放盐能吃的是果子，
地上不撒种能结果的是野地瓜，
山中不栽种能捡来吃的是菌子，
不喂养能拿肉来吃的是野兽鱼虾。
有嘴不说话的是坛子，
无嘴响四方的是唢呐，
知道白天黑夜的是公鸡。
阿姐呀，我说的对不对？
要是说对啦，
我俩做一家！”

"Ah, brother, ah, brother!

What in the world can be eaten without salt?

What can bear fruits without anyone sowing the seeds?

What in the mountains can be eaten without anyone planting it?

Whose meat can be eaten without anyone raising them?

What has a mouth but does not speak?

What does not have a mouth but is heard in all directions?

What knows the day and night?..."

"Sister, sister!

Fruits can be eaten without salt.

Wild sweet potatoes can bear fruits without anyone sowing the seeds.

Mushroom can be picked as food with no one planting it.

Wild animals, fishes and shrimps can be eaten with no one raising them.

Jars have mouths but don't talk.

The suona doesn't have a mouth but can be heard everywhere.

Roosters know day and night.

Sister, am I right?

If I am,

We are husband and wife!"

仙姑眯眯笑，
点头不说话。
他们来到两棵香樟树下，
对着大树磕头作揖。
认一棵树做爹，
认一棵树做娘；
请两棵树作证，
他俩成亲做夫妻。

仙姑娘告诉直眼人，
就选树下作房基，
两人动手盖新房。
妻子去割茅草，
丈夫去砍屋梁。
青石作墙脚，
树枝作椽子，
树叶作瓦片，
树皮当板墙。
两人忙碌了九天，
两人辛苦了九夜，
盖成一间新房。
山雀有窝喳喳叫，
人有住房喜洋洋。

猴子把树果抢吃完了，
他们没有充饥的食粮。
鸟兽把泉水喝干了，
箐里没有泉水流淌。
白狗在门外汪汪哭，

The fairy smiled,
Nodded her head, though remained silent.
They came under the two camphor trees.
Kowtowing and saluting to the trees.
Acknowledging one as farther,
The other as mother,
Letting both trees as their witnesses,
They were married as husband and wife.

The fairy told the vertical-eyed person
To choose the area under a tree as the foundation,
And then the two started building a new house.
The wife went to cut the thatch
While the husband went to cut trees for the beams.
Bluestones were used as the feet of the walls,
Branches as the rafters,
Leaves as the tiles,
Bark as the walls.
The two had worked busily for nine days
And nine nights,
Until the new house was built.
Just as the sparrows sang when they had a nest,
People were happy when they had a house.

The monkeys ate up all the tree fruits
And there was no food anymore.
Birds and wild animals drank up the spring water,
So there was no spring in the bamboo grove.
The white dog cried outside the door,

从白天哭到夜晚，
从夜晚哭到天亮，
哭声震动了诸神王。

涅依倮佐颇召集众神仙，
一齐出主意：
再叫罗塔纪姑娘，
舀来四瓢水，
放进五谷种，
四瓢水泼向大地，
五谷种撒向四方，
地上有了种子，
地上有了雨水。

种子落在大门口，
白狗把种子衔进屋里，
见了仙姑夫妇俩，
摇头摆尾喜的狂。

两夫妇低头看：
“啊，有了种子，
就有食粮；
有了种子啊，
生存就有了希望。”

两人把种子晒了三天，
两人把种子泡了三夜。

From day to night,
From night to day,
Its crying disturbed the immortals.

Nienong Luozuopo
Summoned all the immortals
For another consultation:
They once again asked that Miss Luo Taji
Get four scoops of water,
Put the seeds of the five grains in them,
And then pour the four scoops of water down to the earth,
With the seeds of the five grains scattered in four directions.
There were seeds on the ground,
There was rainwater on the ground.

The seeds fell at the gate and,
The white dog carried them in its mouth to the house.
Seeing the fairy couple,
It shook its head and tail ecstatically.

The couple looked down:
"Ah, with the seeds,
Crops can grow;
With the seeds,
There is hope for survival."

They dried the seeds in the sun for three days
And then soaked the seeds for three nights.

种子撒下地，
一颗发三苗，
一苗生两叶，
幼苗嫩汪汪。

过了一个月，
禾苗绿茵茵，
过了三个月，
谷穗黄生生。
谷子比人高，
一棵谷子生九穗，
一穗谷子有苞谷长。
一丛谷子收九箩，
九箩谷子堆满仓。
苞谷长有房子高，
一棵苞谷背三包，
一包苞谷有手长，
一粒苞谷鸡蛋大，
一棵能收三箩筐。
高粱有大树高，
一棵高粱结三穗，
一穗高粱马尾长，
一颗高粱有核桃大，
一棵高粱收九缸。
夫妇忙收粮，
装满九间房；
夫妇尝新谷，
越吃饭越香。

After the seeds were sown,
Each later sprouted three seedlings,
And each seedling grew two leaves,
What tender seedlings!

After a month,
The seedlings turned green.
After three months,
The ears of millets turned golden.
The millets were taller than people,
With nine ears on each millet plant,
Every ear as big as an ear of corn.
A cluster of the millet filled nine bamboo baskets,
And the baskets of millets filled the barn full.
Each cornstalk was as tall as a house,
Bearing the corn that filled three bags.
A bag of corn was as long as an arm;
A kernel of the corn was as large as an egg;
The kernels of a cornstalk filled three baskets.
The sorghum rose as tall as big tree,
Each bearing three ears,
Each ear as long as a horse's tail,
Each grain as large as a walnut,
So each sorghum stalk filled nine big vats.
The couple was busy harvesting
And filled nine storage rooms;
They tasted the new millets:
The more they ate, the tastier they felt.

二、直眼睛人

撒赛歇和直眼人，
结成夫妻做一家，
日子过得美满，
只愁不生娃娃。

忽然一天夜晚，
仙姑娘肚子疼了，
她生下个皮口袋，
袋里传出咴咴呀呀的声音，
好像娃娃在说话，
不知是男还是女？

撒赛歇听了难过：
“生了个大口袋，
实在羞人啰！”
她看着皮口袋，
从白天哭到夜晚，
从夜晚哭到白天。
哭声传到天上，
被龙王罗阿玛听见，
他派撒赛萨歇姑娘：
“莫伤心啊，莫流泪，
我来看看究竟生了个啥？”

II. Vertical-eyed People

Since Sa Saixie and the vertical-eyed person
Became a couple and formed a family,
Their days were happy
Except that they had no children.

Suddenly one night,
The fairy had an abdomen ache
And then gave birth to a leather bag.
A babbling sound came from the bag,
Like a baby was talking.
Was it a boy or a girl?

Hearing the sound Sa Saixie was sad:
"We give birth to a big bag,
How embarrassing!"
Staring at the leather bag,
She cried from day to night,
From night to day.
The sound of her cry traveled to heaven
And was heard by Dragon Queen Luo Ama,
Who sent Miss Sasai Saxie:
"Do not be sad or shed tears.
Let me see what indeed you gave birth to?"

撒赛萨若埃拿出大剪刀，
把口袋剪成三节，
袋里跳出一群小蚂蚱。
上节四十个，
中节四十个，
下节四十个，
蚂蚱跳三跳，
变成一百二十个胖娃娃。

他们都有两只眼睛，
两只眼睛亮晶晶，
不到一月会说话，
不到二月能走路。
一年就能扛犁耙。
他们是“拉爹”的后代，
他们的名字叫“拉拖”。

一百二十个小“拉拖”，
儿子有六十个，
姑娘有六十个。
儿子大了爱玩泥，
姑娘大了爱采花；
儿子上山开火地，
姑娘河边种桑麻；
儿子长大喜欢姑娘，
姑娘长大催着成家。

Sasai Saruoai took out the big scissors,
And cut the bag into three sections.
Many small grasshoppers jumped out of the bag.
There were forty from the top section,
Forty from the middle section,
Forty from the bottom section.
After three jumps,
They turned into one hundred twenty fat babies.

They all had two eyes,
Bright and shiny eyes.
They all started talking within a month,
Walking within two months,
And shouldering the plow within one year.
They were the offsprings of "La Die".
Their name was "La Tuo".

Of the one hundred and twenty little "La Tuos",
Sixty were their sons and
Sixty were their daughters.
As they grew up, the sons liked to play with mud,
And the daughters loved to pick flowers;
The sons went up to the mountains to set fire and cultivate virgin land,
And the daughters grew mulberry and hemp trees by the river;
The sons grew up and loved girls,
While the daughters grew up and were urged to get married.

世上只有这群兄妹。
兄妹只好成亲做一家。

上节口袋生的四十个，
配成二十家，
去高山种桑麻；
中节口袋生的四十个，
配成二十家，
去坝子种谷、种瓜；
下节口袋生的四十个，
配成二十家，
去河边打鱼捞虾。
兄妹一百二十人，
配成六十家，
一家住一处，
一处一寨隔有篱笆。

过了九千七百年，
世上住不下，
直眼人一天比一天增多，
地方一天比一天窄狭。

直眼睛这代人呀，
他们不懂道理，
他们经常吵嘴打架。
各吃各的饭，
各烧各的汤。
一不管亲友，

They were the only brothers and sisters in the world,
So they had to marry each other and form families.

The forty from the top section of the bag
Made twenty families and
Went up to the mountains to plant mulberry and hemp trees.
The forty from the middle section of the bag,
Made twenty families and
Went to the plains to grow grains and melons.
The forty from the bottom section of the bag
Made twenty families and
Went to the riverside to fish and catch shrimps.
One hundred and twenty siblings,
Made sixty families.
Each family settled in one place,
With fences separating them from each other.

Nine thousand and seven hundred years later,
There was no longer enough space in the world,
For the vertical-eyed people multiplied day by day
And found the space smaller and smaller day by day.

This generation of the vertical-eyed
Was unreasonable.
They often quarreled and fought among themselves.
They ate their meals separately
And made their own soups.
They neither cared about their relatives

二不管爹妈。
爹死了拴着脖子丢在山里，
妈死了拴着脚杆抛进沟凹。

众神之王涅侬倮佐颇，
找来龙王罗阿玛，
水王罗塔纪，
还有古木折意巴①，
一齐来商量：
“树多不砍嘛，
看不见青天；
草多不割嘛，
看不见道路；
不讲道理的人不换嘛，
看不见善良和淳朴。
要重发一代芽，
要重开一次花，
要重结一次果，
要重换一代人。”

神王和仙王，
水王和龙王，
派了涅侬撒萨歇，

① 古木折意巴：又称盘古，参与造天地，重换一代人。

Nor their parents.

When the father died, he was thrown to the mountains with a noose on his neck,

When the mother died, she was thrown into the ditches with a stick on her feet.

The head of immortals Nienong Luozuopo
Summoned Dragon Queen Luo Ama,
Water Queen Luo Taji,
And Gumu Zheyiba①
For another consultation:
"Not felling the overgrown trees,
One cannot see the blue sky;
Not cutting the overgrown grass,
One cannot see the path;
Not replacing the unreasonable people,
One cannot see the kind and honest one.
Let another generation bud,
Another generation flower,
Another generation bear fruit.
Let there be a new generation."

The head of all immortals and Immortal King,
Water Queen and Dragon Queen,
Sent Nienong Sasaxie

---

① Gumu Zheyiba: also called Pangu who participated in creating the heavens, the earth, and the new generation.

查访好心人。
要让好心人传宗接代，
要一代比一代聪明能干，
要一代比一代兴旺发达。

涅侬撒萨歇，
骑着龙马到人间，
走到半路上，
装着跌折龙马腰，
假称跌断龙马腿，
到处找药医龙马。

东方去了去西方，
南方去了去北方，
四方四十大户，
家家都访遍。
每到一家要作一百二十个揖，
每到一户要磕一百二十个头。
“大爹大妈呀，
我的龙马腰折啦，
我的龙马腿断啦，
要人血才能医好，
请阿爹阿妈帮帮忙，
我多多谢你家。”

To look for the kind-hearted person
To have posterity,
Who would grow wiser and more capable generation after generation,
More prosperous generation after generation.

Nienong Sasaxie
Rode the dragon-horse to the world.
Pretending that on his way
His dragon-horse broke its back
And its leg,
He looked everywhere for medicine to cure his dragon-horse.

From east to west,
South to north,
The forty wealthy families in four directions,
He visited them all.
He saluted a hundred and twenty times in each household,
And kowtowed a hundred and twenty times in each household.
"Dear uncle and aunt,
My dragon-horse broke its back
And its leg.
Only the human blood can heal it.
Please, uncle and aunt, please help.
I will be so grateful to you."

四方四大户，
良心又黑又毒辣：
“莫说人血不给你，
人尿也休想给你医龙马。”

涅侬撒萨歇，
离开大户住的寨子，
再次查访好人家。
他走到十字路口，
碰上一个庄稼人。
庄稼人肩上扛着犁，
手中把牛拉。

涅侬撒萨歇，
弯腰又作揖：
“阿哥哟，请你等一等，
问你几句要紧话。”

庄稼人名叫阿朴独姆，
他家里还有一个妹妹。
他看看好心的涅侬撒萨歇，
含笑迎客人：
“过路的阿哥哟，
不用弯腰作揖，
你有难处只管说，
也许我能帮你使点力。”

The four wealthy families in four directions
Were heartless and vicious:
"We would not give you human urine,
Not to mention human blood."

Nienong Sasaxie
Left the cottages of the rich and
Kept looking for the kind-hearted family.
He came to a crossroads,
Where he saw a farmer.
The farmer carried a plow on his shoulder,
Pulling an ox by his hand.

Nienong Sasaxie,
Bowed and saluted:
"Dear brother, could you spare a few minutes please
To talk with me about something important?"

The name of the farmer was Apu Dumu,
Who had a sister at home.
He looked at the kind-hearted Nienong Sasaxie,
Greeted the guest with a smile:
"Brother, the passer-by,
Do not bow or salute,
Just tell me your problem,
And I may be able to help."

“我的龙马腰折啦，
我的龙马腿断啦，
要人血才能医好，
求阿哥帮我医龙马。”

“你把金刀拿给我，
你把银碗拿给我，
划开指头给你血，
若要人肉我也能割下。”
阿朴独姆用金针刺出手上血，
交给涅侬撒萨歇。

涅侬撒萨歇，
拉着阿朴独姆，
对他说了真话：
“我走遍九山十八凹，
没见一个好心人，
没遇一户好人家。
你的心像月亮一样干净，
你为人像大树一样正直，
你是世上最好的人。

“直眼睛这代人，
心肠实在差，
要重换一代人，
要重开一次花。

"My dragon-horse broke its back
And its leg,
Only the human blood can heal it,
So I beg you, brother, please help me heal my dragon-horse."

"Give me the golden knife
And the silver bowl.
I will cut my finger and give you my blood,
Even my flesh if that would help."
Apu Dumu pricked his finger with a golden needle and
Gave the blood to Nienong Sasaxie.

Nienong Sasaxie
Held the hands of Apu Dumu
And told him the truth:
"I went all over the nine mountains and eighteen valleys
But did not meet one kind-hearted person
Or one good family.
Your heart is as clean as the moon,
And you are upright as a tree,
The best person in the world.

"The generation of the vertical-eyed
Is too heartless.
There needs to be a new generation,
A blossom of new flowers.

世上只留你们兄妹传后代，
你们要牢牢记住我的话。

“一百二十天内要发大水，
要用洪水洗大地，
要用洪水洗万物。
洗干净大地，万物再生，
洗干净大地，再种庄稼，
洗干净大地，再传后代。”

The world will have only you and your sister left to propagate:

You must bear these words of mine in mind.

"Within a hundred and twenty days there will be a flood

That will cleanse the earth

And everything on it.

Only after the earth is cleansed can all things renew,

Only after the earth is cleansed can crops regrow,

Only after the earth is cleansed can the human race propagate."

第四章　横眼睛时代

一、洪水滔天

洪水要来了，
地暗又天昏，
月亮无光彩，
太阳无光辉。

阿朴独姆兄妹俩，
听说洪水要淹天，
白天叹息落泪，
黑夜焦愁担心。

涅侬撒萨歇问阿朴独姆：
“好心的庄稼人啊，
为啥焦愁不安？
为啥落泪叹息？”
阿朴独姆回答：
“洪水要来啦，
有金的打金船，

Chapter Four The Era of the Horizontal-eyed

I. The Flood Reaching the Sky

The flood was coming.
It was dark on the earth and faint in the sky.
The moon made dim twilight.
The sun lost its glory.

Apu Dumu and his sister,
Heard that the sky would be flooded.
During the day they sighed and shed tears.
At night they were anxious and worried.

Nienong Sasaxie asked Apu Dumu:
"Kind-hearted farmer,
Why are you worried?
Why are you weeping and sighing?"
Apu Dumu answered:
"Flood is coming.
Build gold boat if you have gold.

有银的打银船，
有铜的打铜船，
有铁的打铁船，
有锡的打锡船。
我们兄妹俩，
没有金银，
没有铜铁，
用什么来打船？
无船怎能躲过洪水，
无船怎能避开灾难？"

涅依撒萨歇说：
"好心的庄稼人，
你不用忧虑，
你不用叹息。
我给你一颗大瓜种，
这颗瓜种不一般，
一半绿来一半红，
拿在日下晒三天，
拿在月下露三晚，
拿去种在家门前。

"栽后三天勤浇水，
栽后七天壅瓜蔓，
栽后十天搭瓜架，
瓜藤架上串枝连。

Build silver boat if you have silver.
Build copper boat if you have copper.
Build iron boat if you have iron.
Build tin boat if you have tin.
Brother and sister,
Neither of us
Has gold or silver,
Copper or iron.
With what can we build a boat?
Without a boat how to escape from flood?
Without a boat how to dodge calamity?"

Nienong Sashaxie said:
"Kind-hearted farmer,
You neither need to worry
Nor to sigh.
I give you a big melon seed,
With magic power,
Green and red in half.
Dry it in the sun for three days.
Bathe it in the moonlight for three nights.
Plant it in front of the door of your house."

"Water it frequently for three days after being planted.

Cover the seed with soil and wait for sprourting for seven days after being planted.

Put up melon rack ten days after being planted.

Melon vines twist with each other on the rack.

瓜藤横爬十八拿，
瓜藤直爬接通天。
藤上结个大葫芦，
你们和葫芦有因缘。

“三月种瓜子，
六月葫芦就长成，
九月葫芦皮变黄，
十月葫芦硬又坚。
腊月摘葫芦，
葫芦有房子大，
挖空葫芦就是船，
你们兄妹住中间。”

阿朴独姆，
心事想不完：
“有了躲洪水的地方，
还缺吃的又怎么办？”

涅侬撒萨歇，
开言又指点：
“给你一碗粮，
千万莫吃完，
今日吃了明日长，
明日吃了又还原，
永远吃不完。

Melon vines extend horizontally for eighteen pai①.
Melon vine climbs vertically into sky.
A gourd grows on the vine.
You are doomed to have it."

"In March melon seed is planted.
In June it bears a gourd.
In September it turns yellow.
In October it grows hard.
In December it is picked.
The gourd is as big as a house,
Just like a boat after being caverned.
You two live in it."

Apu Dumu
Was still worried:
"We get the place to escape from flood,
Then how about food shortage?"

Nienong Sashaxie,
Talked again and instructed:
"Give you a bowl of grain.
Don't eat it up.
You eat part of it today and the rest grows tomorrow.

You will eat it tomorrow and it will turn back into a full bowl of grain.

You will never finish it off."

---

① pai: a unit of length equal to the arm span of an adult.

“再给你一把种子，
你们要勤耕苦种田。
庄稼遍地长，
粮食吃不完。”

阿朴独姆兄妹俩，
把话记心间。
藏着种子带着粮，
钻进葫芦里面。

勤快的小蜜蜂，
衔来黄蜂蜡，
把葫芦的口封严，
使兄妹俩免遭水淹。

涅侬撒萨歇，
看着他们躲进葫芦里，
心中扎实喜欢。
他才吩咐老龙下大雨，
要下得洪水淹到天边。

龙眼眨一眨，
满天乌云翻；
龙尾摆一摆，
天空就扯闪；
龙身抖一抖，
狂风暴雨卷万山。

"Give you another handful of seeds.
Work on the farm diligently.
Crops would grow all over the ground.
The grain will be inexhaustible."

Apu Dumu, the brother and sister,
Bearing the words in mind,
Hid seeds, carried the grain and,
Crept into the gourd.

Diligent little bee,
Held yellow beeswax in its mouth and,
Sealed off the gourd,
In case that the brother and sister suffered from the flood.

Nienong Sashaxie,
Seeing them creeping into the gourd,
Felt pretty relieved.
Then he ordered the old dragon to start the rainfall,
Which would bring flood to the edge of the sky.

In a blink of the dragon,
Black clouds gathered all over the sky.
In a swing of the tail of the dragon,
Lightning crackled through the sky.
In a shake of the body of the dragon,
Violent storms whipped mountains.

雨点鸡蛋大，
雨柱似竹竿；
下了七天七夜，
大地茫茫被水淹。
地上波浪滚滚，
波涛直冲云天。

树根飘上天，
浮萍天上转，
乱草裹成团，
天连水，
水连天，
葫芦飘到天上边。

大鱼想吃星星，
黄鳝在天上乱钻；
石蚌望着月亮乱叫，
虾子围着星星撒欢；
水鸭在天空漫游，
水獭在天际打圈圈。

金船沉海底，
银船沉海底，
铜船沉海底，
铁船、锡船也沉海底。

Raindrops were as big as eggs.
Rain columns were as thick as bamboo poles.
The rain lasted for seven days and nights.
Vast land was flooded.
Waves rolled along in a succession on the ground.
Waves thrust up into sky.

Tree roots floated in the air.
Duckweed whirled in the sky.
Weeds rolled into balls.
Sky and water are in one piece and
Cannot be separated,
The gourd flied high up in the sky.

Big fish wanted to eat stars.
Eels ran helter-skelter in the sky.
Stone frogs barked at moon.
Shrimps gamboled around stars.
Ducks roamed in the air.
Otters circled in the sky.

Gold boat sank to the bottom of the sea.
Silver boat sank to the bottom of the sea.
Copper boat sank to the bottom of the sea.
Iron boat and tin boat sank to the bottom of the sea.

涅依倮佐颇，
召集众神仙来商量：
派涅依撒萨歇，
派罗塔纪姑娘，
还有古木折意巴，
共同治洪水。

古木折意巴，
想出办法治洪水：
东方水门开，
南方水门开，
西方水门开，
北方水门开，
四方水门开，
大水还是淌不干。

他叫来白尾巴乌鸦：
“你去叫石蚌蹬开山口，
叫石蚌踢开水眼；
让洪水从山口流走，
让洪水从水眼淌完。”

洪水逐渐降落，
可是落水太慢。
涅依撒萨歇，
罗塔纪姑娘，
古木折意巴，
一齐来巡察。

Nienong Luozuopo,
Called gods together for discussion:
Sent Nienong Sashaxie,
Sent the Miss Luo Taji,
And Gumu Zheyiba,
To control the flood together.

Gumu Zheyiba,
Found a way to control the flood:
Open the east water gate.
Open the south water gate.
Open the west water gate.
Open the north water gate.
Open the four directions water gates.
The water still could not be drained.

He summoned the white-tail crow:
"You go and ask stone frogs to kick open the mountain pass.
Ask stone frogs to kick open the water hole;
Let the flood go through the mountain pass.
Let the flood go through the water hole."

The level of flood water descended,
But the speed was too low.
Nienong Sashaxie,
Miss Luo Taji
Gumu Zheyiba,
Made an inspection together.

古木折意巴，
再派白尾巴乌鸦，
飞去喊太阳，
飞去喊月亮。

白尾巴乌鸦放声唤：
“太阳快出来！
月亮快出来！
月亮和太阳，
不理睬白尾巴乌鸦。

罗塔纪姑娘，
再派白老鹰，
叫它飞到太阳落处，
叫它飞到月亮落处，
把日月衔起来。
白尾巴老鹰最听话，
它把太阳衔出来，
它把月亮衔出来。

他们派太阳来晒水，
他们派月亮来烤河川。
太阳火辣辣，
月亮亮闪闪，
晒了九天九夜，
烤了九天九夜，
洪水落了九天九夜。

Gumu Zheyiba
Sent the white-tail crow again
To call the sun and
To call the moon.

The white-tail crow shouted:
"Come out, sun!
Come out, moon!"
The sun and the moon
Ignored the white-tail crow.

Miss Luo Taji
Sent the white eagle again.
She asked it to fly to the sun setting place and,
The moon setting place,
To hold the sun and the moon in its mouth.
The white-tail eagle was the most obedient one.
It held the sun in its beak and dragged it out.
It held the moon in its beak and dragged it out.

They sent the sun to dry the water.
They sent the moon to scorch the river.
The sun was burning and
Dried the water for nine days and nights.
The moon was shining and
Scorched the rivers for nine days and nights.
The flood lasted for nine days and nights.

洪水落了三尺，
洪水落了九千丈，
葫芦也落了九千丈；
现出了山峦，
露出了平原，
树尖冒新芽，
地上草再生。

岩边有三蓬树；
一蓬细篾树，
一蓬尖刀树，
一蓬小竹树。
三种树相交错，
三种树紧相连，
三种树搭成棚，
三种树遮住天。

葫芦往下落，
落在竹树间，
树枝竹梢缠紧葫芦，
把葫芦拴在岩边。

The depth of flood decreased by three Chi①.
The depth of flood decreased by nine thousand Zhang②.
The gourd fell by nine thousand Zhang.
Mountains emerged from water.
Plains were revealed.
New leaves sprouted from the trees.
Grass revived on the land.

Three clumps of trees grew from the edge of cliff;
One clump was with slender strip leaves.
One clump was with sharp-knife-shape leaves.
One clump was small bamboo tree.
Three clumps interlocked with each other.
Three clumps joined together.
Three clumps put up a shed.
Three clumps blotted out the sky.

The gourd fell off and
Landed in the bamboo grove.
The gourd was entangled by branches and the tips of bamboo,
And tied to the cliff.

---

① Chi: a unit of length equal to one-third meter.

② Zhang: a unit of length equal to 3 and 1/3 meter.

二、找葫芦

洪水洗净了大地，
洪水洗净了万物。
涅侬撒萨歇，
为找大葫芦，
寻人传人烟，
又来到了人间。

涅侬撒萨歇啊，
从高山找到平坝，
从平坝找上高山。
迎面遇上老土蜂，
笑着把话问：
“土蜂、土蜂你到处飞，
咯见着大葫芦？
葫芦上还糊有黄蜡，
两兄妹就藏在里面。”

土蜂忙回答：
“没有见着大葫芦，
没有见到两兄妹。
要是见着嘛，
糊葫芦的黄蜡，
我早把它吃完。”

II. Searching for the Gourd

The flood washed up the earth.
The flood washed up the world.
Nienong Sashaxie,
In order to search for the big gourd,
And people to expand human habitation,
Came to the world.

Aha, Nienong Sashaxie,
Searched from high mountains to plains,
From plains to high mountains.
He encountered an old scoliid,
Smiled and asked:
"Scoliid, scoliid, you fly to everywhere,
Er, did you see the big gourd?
Yellow beeswax is plastered on the big gourd.
The brother and sister hide in it."

The scoliid answered immediately:
"I have never met any big gourd.
I have never seen any brother or sister.
If I got it,
The gourd plasterd with yellow beewax,
I would eat it up."

涅侬撒萨歇，
怒火涌心间：
“土蜂的心肠坏，
土蜂的嘴太馋。
要叫后代人，
用火烧死你！”
从此以后嘌，
彝家见了老土蜂，
用火烧它才心甘。

涅侬撒萨歇，
继续往前看，
迎面来了葫芦包①
“葫芦包啊葫芦包，
你到处飞舞，
“老鼠、老鼠你到处钻，
嗰见个大葫芦？
嗰见着两兄妹？”

葫芦包嗡嗡叫：
“没有见着大葫芦，
也没见到两兄妹。
要是见着嘛，
我要叮死他，
饱饱吃一餐。”

① 葫芦包：一种野蜂的名称。

Nienong Sashaxie,
Burst into anger and said:
"Scoliid, you are so vicious.
Scoliid, you are so greedy.
Let your offspring
Set you on fire!"
Hey, from then on,
Whenever Yi people met the old scoliid,
They would burn it.

Nienong Sashaxie,
Continued to look forwards and
Encountered a vespula.
"Vespula①, aha, vespula
You fly to everywhere.
Have you ever seen the big gourd?
Have you ever seen the brother and sister?"

The vespula was humming:
"I have never seen any big gourd,
Nor have I seen any brother or sister.
If I got them,
I would sting them to death,
And have a big meal."

① Vespula: the name of a kind of wild bee.

涅依撒萨歇，
气得冒火烟：
“狠心的小东西，
心肠这么坏。
后代只配头朝下，
吊死才心甘。”
从此以后嘤，
葫芦包的子孙，
个个的头朝下悬。

涅依撒萨歇，
继续往前看，
迎面来了小老鼠。
“老鼠、老鼠你到处钻，
略见着大葫芦？
葫芦里面有水，
葫芦里面有粮，
葫芦里面有两兄妹。”

小老鼠唧唧叫：
“没有见着大葫芦，
也没见到两兄妹。
要是见到了，
葫芦里的粮食，
我早把它吃完。”

Nienong Sashaxie,
Was fumed with anger and said:
"You cruel little guy,
You are so blackhearted.
Your offspring will be heels over head
And be hanged to death."
Hey, from then on,
Offspring of vespula,
Each hangs upside down.

Nienong Sashaxie,
Continued to look forwards and
Encountered a little mouse.
"Mouse, mouse, you go through everywhere.
Have you ever seen the big gourd?
There is water in it.
There is grain in it.
There are the brother and sister in it.

Little mouse chirred:
"I have never met any big gourd,
I have never seen any brother or sister,
If I got them,
The grain in the gourd
Would be eaten up by me."

涅侬撒萨歇，
气得眼瞪圆：
“贪嘴的小东西，
数你讨人嫌！
后代人见了你，
人人揍你才喜欢。”
从此以后嘿，
老鼠一出现，
人人喊打不迟延。

涅侬撒萨歇，
继续往前赶。
迎面遇上小绿雀。
“小绿雀啊小绿雀，
你成天到处飞；
略见着大葫芦，
略见着两兄妹？”

小绿雀点头忙回答：
“没有见着大葫芦，
没有见着两兄妹。
要是见到了，
我找粮食给他们吃。”

涅侬撒萨歇，
听了很喜欢：
“巧嘴的小绿雀，

Nienong Sashaxie,
Glared angrily at it:
"Gluttonous little guy,
You are a swine.
Whenever future generations meet you,
They would like to beat you."
Hey, from then on,
Once the mouse appeared,
People would not hesitate to yell and beat.

Nienong Sashaxie,
Continued to walk forwards and
Encountered a little green finch.
"Little green finch, little green finch, you fly to everywhere.
Have you ever seen the big gourd?
Have you ever seen the brother and sister?"

The little green finch nodded its head and hastened to answer:
"I have never met any big gourd,
I have never seen any brother or sister,
If I met them,
I would look for grain
To feed them."

Nienong Sashaxie,
Listened and felt pleased:
"Clever little green finch,

你的心肠好，
庄稼熟了你先尝。”
从此以后嘿
世上小绿雀，
田里新谷它先尝。

涅侬撒萨歇，
继续往前走，
迎面遇着老喜鹊：
“喜鹊啊喜鹊，
你成天到处飞，
略见着个大葫芦，
略见着兄妹俩？”

喜鹊喳喳叫：
“没有见着大葫芦，
没有见着兄妹俩。
要是见着嘛，
早就飞来把喜讯传。”

涅侬撒萨歇，
听了心里甜：
“好心的喜鹊呀，
今后请你住屋前。
客人来了你早知道，
时时听见你把喜讯传。”
从此以后嘿，
喜鹊房前来做窝，
站在枝头唱得欢。

You are kind-hearted,
You taste first when the crops are ripe."
Hey, from then on,
Little green finches in the world,
Would taste the new grain in the fields first.

Nienong Sashaxie,
Continued to walk forwards and
Encountered an old magpie:
"Magpie, magpie,
You fly to everywhere all day long.
Have you ever seen the big gourd?
Have you ever seen the brother and sister?"

The magpie chirped:
"I have never met any big gourd.
I have never seen any brother or sister.
If I met them,
I would fly to send the good news."

Nienong Sashaxie,
Listened and rejoiced:
"Kind-hearted magpie,
Please live in front of people's houses hereafter.
You will be the first one to know the guests' visiting.
You will send good news every day."
Hey, from then on,
Magpies make nests in front of houses,
Caroling cheerfully on branches.

涅依撒萨歇，
继续往前走，
迎面来了小蜜蜂。
“小蜜蜂啊小蜜蜂，
你一生勤劳不偷闲；
你采百花到山间，
你喀见着个大葫芦，
你喀见着两兄妹？”

小蜜蜂嗡嗡唱：
“我见到了大葫芦，
我见到了两兄妹。
在东边高山上，
有座白岩山；
白岩山边三蓬树，
一蓬细篾树，
一蓬小竹树，
一蓬尖刀树，
三种枝叶紧相连，
三种枝叶遮住天，
大葫芦就挂在枝头间。”

涅依撒萨歇，
听罢笑开颜，
“辛勤的小蜜蜂，
世上百花任你采，
四季鲜花你先尝。
鲜花酿蜜香又甜，

Nienong Sashaxie,
Continued to walk forwards and
Encountered a little bee:
"Little bee, little bee,
You work hard and never slack off all your life.
You gather honey from flowers in mountains.
Have you ever seen the big gourd?
Have you ever seen the brother and sister?"

The little bee buzzed:
"I have seen the big gourd,
I have seen the brother and sister.
Among the mountains in the east,
There is a white rock mountain.
Three clumps of trees grow beside it.
One clump is with slender strip leaves.
One clump is small bamboo tree.
One clump is with sharp-knife-shape leaves.
Three clumps of branches interlock with each other.
Three clumps of leaves blot out the sky.
The gourd is hung up on the branches."

Nienong Sashaxie,
Listened and smiled,
"Busy little bee,
Flowers of all sorts are at your disposal,
Flowers of four seasons will be tasted first by you.
Honey gathered from flowers is fragrant and sweet.

人类子孙喂养你，
请你住进屋里面。”
从此以后嘿，
百花丛中的小蜜蜂，
人人见了都喜欢。

三、配亲

涅侬撒萨歇，
找到了大葫芦，
打葫芦口，
走出阿朴独姆两兄妹。

洪水已经退了，
大地一片荒寂。
百里无草木，
千里无鸟兽，
万里无人烟。

哥哥看了焦虑，
妹妹看了哭泣：
“家中鸡没有，
家中狗没有；
独有我兄妹，
咋个做人家？”
涅侬撒萨歇，

The offspring of human beings will feed you and,
Invite you to live in their houses."
Hey, from then on,
Little bees that fly among the flowers,
Are loved by everyone.

III. Matchmaking

Nienong Sashaxie,
Found the big gourd and,
Opened it.
The Apu Dumu brother and sister walked out of it.

The flood retreated.
The land was in desolate silence.
No plant grew in a hundred li① round.
No birds or wild animals inhabited in a thousand li round.
No people lived in ten thousand li round.

The brother saw everything and was anxious.
The sister saw everything and cried:
"No chicken at home,
No dog at home;
Only us, the brother and sister,
How to make up a family?"
Nienong Sashaxie,

① li: a unit of length equal to 500 meters.

指点阿朴独姆：
“要让世上有人烟，
你们兄妹做夫妻。”

兄妹听了心中急，
兄妹怎能做夫妻？！

涅侬撒萨歇，
想了个好主意：
“兄妹能否做夫妻，
你们滚东西试一试。”

他拿来了簸箕，
又拿来了筛子，
交给兄妹俩：
“两件东西分离；
你们不做夫妻；
两件东西合拢，
你们就做夫妻。”

哥哥拿筛子上南山，
妹妹拿簸箕上北坡；
簸箕、筛子同时滚，
滚到箐底合一起。
妹妹看了低下头，

Instructed Apu Dumu:
"In order to make the land populated,
You brother and sister should be husband and wife."

Hearing that the brother and sister were worried.
How can brother and sister become husband and wife?!

Nienong Sashaxie,
Came up with a good idea:
"You can try rolling something.
It will tell you whether brother and sister can be a couple or not."

He brought a flat wicker tray,
And a sieve.
He gave them to the brother and sister:
"If the two things are separated,
You will not be husband and wife.
If two things join together,
You will be a couple."

The brother took the sieve up to the south mountain.
The sister took the flat wicker tray up to the north slope.
The flat wicker tray and the sieve rolled down the mountain at the same time and,
Joined together at the bottom of the bamboo grove.
Seeing that, the sister lowered her head.

哥哥看了不出气①。

涅侬撒萨歇说：
“簸箕、筛子合一起，
兄妹能够做夫妻！”

阿朴独姆兄妹说：
“碰巧滚一块，
兄妹不能做夫妻。”

涅侬撒萨歇，
搬来一盘磨。
哥抬上扇去东山，
妹背下扇去西山，
两扇一齐滚下坡，
滚到箐底合一起。

涅侬撒萨歇说：
“石磨合在一起，
兄妹能够做夫妻。”

阿朴独姆回答：
“碰巧滚在一起，
还是不能做夫妻。”

① 不出气：不说话。

Seeing that, the brother held his breath①.

Nienong Sashaxie said:
"Since the flat wicker tray and the sieve join together.
The brother and sister can be husband and wife!"

The Apu Dumu brother and sister said:
"They join together by accident.
Brother and sister cannot be husband and wife."

Nienong Sashaxie,
Fetched a millstone.
The brother carried the upper millstone to the east mountain.
The sister carried the lower millstone to the west mountain.
The two millstones rolled down the slopes at the same time and
Joined together at the bottom of the bamboo grove.

Nienong Sashaxie said:
"Since the millstones join together,
The brother and sister can be husband and wife!"

Apu Dumu answered:
"They join together by accident.
Brother and sister still cannot be husband and wife."

---

① held his breath: was silent, did not talk.

涅依撒萨歇，
取来针和线，
哥哥拿丝线站河头，
妹妹拿花针去河尾，
针线同时丢进河里，
冲到河滩看仔细，
丝线穿进花针里。

涅依撒萨歇
拍手笑嘻嘻：
“三件东西试三次，
三次相合在一起，
水顺沟流道理在，
你俩应当做夫妻。”

阿朴独姆兄妹俩，
羞得把头低，
无法再推辞，
只好答应做夫妻。

四、民族的来源

阿朴独姆兄妹成亲后，
生下三十六个小娃娃。
十八棵青冈树①，

① 青冈树：指男孩，下句的马缨花，指女孩。

Nienong Sashaxie,
Fetch a needle and a thread.
The brother took the thread to the head of river.
The sister took the needle to the end of river.
The needle and thread were thrown into the river at the same time.
They went and watched carefully on the benchland:
The thread went through the eye of the needle.

Nienong Sashaxie,
Clapped hands and laughed:
"Three things have been tried for three times.
For three times they joined together.
The truth is obvious that
You two should become husband and wife."

The Apu Dumu brother and sister,
Lowered their heads bashfully.
Unable to decline,
They had to agree to be husband and wife.

IV. The Origin of the Ethnic Group

After the marriage of the Apu Dumu brother and sister,
They gave birth to thirty-six babies:
Eighteen baby boys like Oriental white oaks① and

① Oriental white oaks: refer to boys. Lantana flowers in the next sentence refer to girls.

十八朵马缨花，
他们两眼横着生，
他们都是小哑巴。
天天围在火塘边，
只是烤火不会说话。

涅侬撒萨歇，
想出办法医哑巴。
叫爹妈砍来竹子，
放在火塘里烧炸。
只听竹子叭叭响，
这个叫“阿噝噝”，
那个叫“阿喳喳”，
有的叫“啊呀呀”……
哑巴从此会说话。

一个抢锄头往东跑，
一个抢扁担往西跑，
三十六个好儿女，
各走一方分了家。

“阿嗞嗞”是彝语，
成了今天的彝家；
“阿喳喳”是哈尼语，
哈尼的祖先就是他；
“啊呀呀”是汉语，
他成了后来的汉家。

Eighteen baby girls like Lantana flowers.
The babies had two horizontal eyes.
They were dumb kids.
They surrounded the fireplace,
Warmed themselves and never talked.

Nienong Sashaxie,
Figured out a way to cure the dumb kids.
He asked the parents to fetch bamboos,
And burnt them in the fireplace.
With cracking sounds,
One child shouted "ah zi zi",
One child shouted "ah zha zha" and
Another shouted "ah ya ya"...
From then on, the dumb kids started to talk.

One carried a hoe running to the east.
One carried a shoulder pole running to the west.
Thirty-six sons and daughters,
Went in different directions and lived apart.

"Ah zi zi" is Yi language.
The people who spoke it are ancestors of Yi people.
"Ah zha zha" is Hani language.
The people who spoke it are ancestors of Hani people;
"Ah ya ya" is Han language.
The people who spoke it are ancestors of Han people;

抢锄头的是彝族，
抢扁担的是傣家；
彝族山头烧火地，
傣家挑担住平坝。
从此各人为一族，
三十六族分天下；
三十六族常来往，
和睦相处是一家。

世上有了人烟，
世上分了民族，
他们要生存繁衍，
他们要认识事物。
他们怎样开创历史，
他们又怎样创造万物？
彝家的兄弟啊，
请听后面的根谱。

The ones carried hoes were Yi people.
The ones carried shoulder poles were Dai people.
Yi people set fire and cultivated virgin land on mountaintops.
And Dai people carried shoulder poles and settled on plains.
Since then they became separated ethnic groups.
Thirty-six groups came into being in the world.
Thirty-six groups were in contact with each other and,
Lived harmoniously as family members.

There were signs of human habitation in the world.
There were different ethnic groups in the world.
They need to live and reproduce.
They need to know things.
How did they make history?
How did they create everything?
Brothers of Yi people,
Let's listen to the following history of our ancestors.

下　部

Volume Two

第一章 麻和棉

一、种麻

大江边住着的白彝人，
是阿朴独姆的后裔，
房子多得像蜂窝，
人多得像蚂蚁，
就是没有衣裳穿，
大家心头都很着急。

歇索的三个儿子，
想出了个主意：
弯刀拿在手中，
斧子别在腰里，
去到大山头，
砍树种旱地。

斧子砍大树，
弯刀砍小树，
木渣四方溅，
就像蝴蝶飞舞。

Chapter One Flax and Cotton

I. Planting Flax

On the bank of great river lived Bai Yi people,
The offspring of Apu Dumu.
Houses were as many as beehives.
People were as many as ants.
All of them were anxious,
Because they had no clothes to wear.

Three sons of Xie Suo,
Came up with an idea:
With cutlasses in hands,
With axes on waist,
They went into mountains,
To cut trees and cultivate crops on dry land.

Cut down big trees with axes.
Chopped down little trees with cutlasses.
Sawdust rose and flew in the sky,
Just like butterflies.

一连砍三天，
砍完一座山。
地上烧大火，
火焰冲上天。
三天火不熄，
烧了九座山，
遍地是草灰，
山头黑一片。

歇索的三个儿子，
回到了家中，
问爹妈和哥嫂，
要种什么庄稼？
阿爹说："要撒油菜籽。"
阿妈说："要撒芝麻籽。"
阿哥阿嫂说："要撒大麻籽。"
歇索的三个儿子，
阿爹的话要听，
阿妈的话有理，
阿哥阿嫂的话也可取。
公鸡不叫就起来，
大哥挑水，
大嫂煮米，
鸡叫忙吃饭，
带上荞粑粑和工具，
太阳一出就上山，
山头撒油菜，
山腰撒芝麻，
山下撒大麻籽。

They kept cutting for three days in a row.
They finished cutting the trees of a mountain.
Fire burned on land.
Flame rose up into sky.
The fire did not die out in three days.
Nine mountains were burnt.
Grass ash was everywhere.
Mountaintops were all in black.

Three sons of Xie Suo,
Went back home, and
Asked parents, brother and sister-in-law:
What crops would they plant?
Father said: "sow rapeseeds."
Mother said: "sow sesame seeds."
Brother and sister-in-law said: "sow linseeds."
Three sons of Xie Suo,
Should follow father's words,
Should obey mother's order and
Listen to the reasonable suggestion of brother and sister-in-law.
Getting up before cock crowed,
Brother went to fetch water.
Sister-in-law cooked rice.
Breakfast was finished right away after cock's crow.
Buckwheat pancakes and tools were carried.
They made their way up the mountain as soon as sun rose.
Rapeseeds were sown on the mountaintop.
Sesame seeds were sown on the mountainside.
Linseeds were sown at the mountain foot.

过了两个月，
爹妈叫哥嫂去看地，
哥嫂叫三兄弟去看地，
歇索的三个儿子，
来到地边上，
大麻长的房子高，
油菜开花遍地黄，
芝麻开花飘白絮。

又过了三个月，
大麻秆长得白和生，
油菜籽结得压弯秆，
芝麻籽结满枝。
阿爹割油菜，
阿妈割芝麻，
阿嫂割大麻，
收割庄稼心欢喜。

歇索的家里，
菜籽堆满一屋子，
芝麻堆满一屋子，
大麻堆满一屋子。
爹妈望着笑眯眯，
哥嫂望着笑嘻嘻。

Two months passed,

Parents asked brother and sister-in-law to check the crops.

Brother and sister-in-law asked the three brothers to check the crops.

Three sons of Xie Suo,

Came to the farmland.

Flax grew as high as houses.

Rape flowers were yellowing the fields.

Sesame flowers blossomed with white oakum flying.

Another three months passed,

Flax stalks looked white and fresh.

Rapeseed stalks were bowed down with the weight of its fruits.

The branches were full of sesame seeds.

Father reaped rapeseeds.

Mother harvested sesames.

Sister-in-law cropped flax.

Everyone rejoiced at the harvest.

At Xie Suo's home,

One room was full of rapeseeds.

One room was full of sesames.

One room was full of flax.

Parents looked at them happily.

Brother and sister-in-law looked and smiled.

阿哥白天剥麻皮，
阿嫂夜晚把麻搓细，
绩成麻线织成布，
全家穿上麻布衣。

阿爹白天剥麻皮，
阿妈晚上搓麻绳，
搓成麻绳织成网，
拿着江上去打鱼。

剩下的拿去街上卖，
卖得金银买家具。
江边白彝人，
日子过得还富裕。
穿上自织麻布衣，
织网种地又猎渔。

二、种棉

麻布衣裳有了，
棉布衣服还没有。

哪个来种棉？
哪个来纺纱？
哪个来织布？
哪个来染花？

Brother peeled off the skin of flax in the daytime.
Sister-in-law twisted flax into threads at night.
Twisted flaxen threads were weaved into linen cloth.
All the family put on linen clothes.

Father peeled off the skin of flax in the daytime.
Mother twisted flaxen strings at night.
Twisted flaxen strings were weaved into net.
They carried it onto rivers to catch fish.

Remaining strings were sold on the street.
The silver and gold earned were used to buy furniture.
Bai Yi people by rivers,
Wearing linen clothes made by themselves,
Weaving, farming and fishing,
Lived a fairly rich life.

II. Planting Cotton

Linen clothes came into being,
But cotton clothes did not yet.

Who planted cotton?
Who did spinning?
Who weaved cloth?
Who dyed cloth?

歇索的三个儿子，
晚上搓麻绳，
白天上山支扣子。
山头支副扣子，
山腰支副扣架，
山脚支副扣架。

过了三天去查看：
山顶那一扣，
麂子挣断扣索；
山腰那一扣，
麝子没勒着；
山脚那一扣，
没有扣住山鸡脚。

三兄弟想了想：
菜籽抓一把，
麻籽抓一把，
芝麻抓一把。
山顶扣子下面撒菜籽，
山腰扣子下面撒芝麻，
山脚扣子下面撒麻籽。

Three sons of Xie Suo,
Twisted flaxen strings at night and
Went up the mountain and laid three traps in the daytime.
One trap was laid on the mountaintop.
One trap was laid on the mountainside.
One trap was laid at the mountain foot.

Three days later they went to check:
Muntjac broke the trap
On the mountaintop.
Musk deer extricated itself from the trap
On the mountainside.
Pheasant escaped from the trap
At the mountain foot.

The three brothers thought over:
They took a handful of rapeseeds.
They took a handful of linseeds.
They took a handful of sesames seeds.

Rapeseeds were scattered on the ground under the trap on the mountaintop.

Sesames seeds were scattered on the ground under the trap on the mountainside.

Linseeds were scattered on the ground under the trap at the mountain foot.

又过两天去查看：
山顶那一扣，
没扣着麂子；
山腰那一扣，
没扣着麝子；
山腰那一扣，
扣着只大孔雀。
孔雀很好看：
头上红三道，
身穿五彩衣，
身上绿三道，
翅膀铜钱花，
尾巴像蝴蝶，
开屏像彩霞。

歇索的三个儿子，
把孔雀带回家。
爹妈见了问：
“这个是什么鸟啊？
头上三道红。”
哥嫂见了问：
“这个是什么鸟啊？
身上三道花。”
姑娘见了问：
“到底是什么鸟啊？
尾巴像蝴蝶，
翅膀铜钱花。”

Two days later they went to check.
The trap on the mountaintop
Did not catch any muntjac.
The trap on the mountainside
Did not catch any musk deer.
The trap at the mountain foot
Did catch a big peacock.
The peacock looked beautiful:
Three red stripes on head,
Five colors in coat,
Three green stripes on body,
Copper coin flowers on wings,
The tail like a butterfly
And rosy clouds when spread out.

The three sons of Xie Suo,
Brought the peacock back home.
Parents saw it and asked:
"Three stripes on head.
What kind of bird it is?"
Brother and sister-in-law saw it and asked:
"Three stripes on body.
What kind of bird it is?"
Girl saw it and asked:
"The tail is like a butterfly.
With copper coin flowers on wings,
What kind of bird it exactly is?"

阿哥忙回答:
“山中最美的马缨花,
鸟中最美的是花孔雀,
今天是吉祥的孔雀到我家。”

歇索的三个儿子,
剖开孔雀头,
不见脑浆只有三颗棉花籽;
剖开孔雀心,
没有心血只有三颗棉花籽;
破开孔雀骨,
没有骨髓只有三颗棉花籽;
取出九颗棉花籽,
交给阿爹阿妈。
阿爹拿着喜欢,
阿妈看着高兴,
把它藏在柜旮旯。

布谷鸟枝头叫,
撒种的时候到啦!
爹妈从柜里取出棉籽,
土掌房上晒一下。

歇索的三个儿子,
来到地里种棉花。
阿嫂撒种子,
阿哥弄犁耙,

Brother answered at once:

"The most beautiful flower in the mountain is Lantana flower.

The most beautiful bird is the colorful peacock.

Today the auspicious peacock came to my house."

Three sons of Xie Suo
Cut open peacock's head,
In which they found no brains but three cotton seeds.
Peacock's heart was cut open,
In which there was no heart blood but three cotton seeds.
Peacock's bone was cut open,
In which there was no marrow but three cotton seeds.
Nine cotton seeds were taken out,
And handed to parents.
Father was pleased to hold them.
Mother looked at them and smiled.
They hid them in the nook of cabinet.

Cuckoo began calling on the branch.
It's time to sow!
Parents took cotton seeds out of the cabinet,
Put them on the soil palm house and dried them in the sun.

Three sons of Xie Suo,
Came to the farmland to plant cotton.
Sister-in-law scattered seeds.
Brother pulled plough.

清明撒下种，
谷雨抽嫩芽。

过了一个月，
哥嫂去瞧棉花，
棉苗绿油油，
一棵棉苗五个杈。

又过三个月，
棉苗长得又高又大，
棉桃压枝头，
棉田白花花。

歇索一家人，
忙着收棉花。
棉花堆满一屋，
满屋都是花。
歇索家会种棉，
消息传遍天下，
乡亲们赶来看，
十人看了九人夸。

歇索老爹问大家：
“哪个会纺纱？

Seeds were sowed in the Qingming Festival.
Seedlings sprouted on Grain Rain①.

One month passed.
Brother and sister-in-law went to check cotton.
Cotton seedlings were glossy and green.
Five branches grew on each seedling.

Three months passed.
The seedlings were tall and thick.
The branches were weighed down by cotton balls.
Cotton field was in endless whiteness.

The Xie Suo family,
Was busy with harvesting cotton.
Cotton was piled up in the house.
The house was full of cotton.
The Xie Suo family knew how to plant cotton.
The news spread all over the world.
Villagers came to see.
Nine in ten people would speak highly of it.

Daddy Xie Suo asked people:
"Who can do spinning?

① Grain Rain: It is the sixth solar term in the twenty-four solar terms. When this day comes, the amount of rainfall increases which is very important for the growth of the crops.

哪个会织布?”
德白西回答:
“我会纺纱。”
哈若西回答:
“我会织布。”
歇索一家听了欢喜,
乡亲们听了高兴,
有的吹起芦笙,
有的吹起唢呐,
就请德白西纺纱,
就请哈若西织布。

德白西白天纺纱,
哈若西晚上织布。
德白西把棉花纺成了纱,
哈若西用纱线织成纱帕。

棉布是织出来了,
缺少光泽颜色差。
歇索的三个儿子,
到街上买染料。
他们从街头找到街尾,
染料满街挂。
红黑黄蓝样样有,
绚丽似彩霞。

Who can weave cloth?"
De Baixi answered:
"I can spin."
Ha Ruoxi answered:
"I can weave cloth."
Hearing this, the Xie Suo family rejoiced.
Hearing this, the villagers were pleased.
Someone blew Lusheng.
Someone blew Suona.
De Baixi was invited to spin.
Ha Ruoxi was invited to weave cloth.

De Baixi spun in the daytime.
Ha Ruoxi weaved cloth at night.
De Baixi spun yarn from cotton.
Ha Ruoxi weaved yarn into cloth.

Cotton cloth came out,
But lacked gloss and color.
The three sons of Xie Suo,
Went to the street to buy dyes.
They searched from one end of the street to the other.
Dyes were hung all over the street.
Red, black, yellow, blue and all other colors,
Which were as colorful as rosy clouds,
Were all obtainable.

各样颜料买三斤，
急急忙忙拿回家。

德白西染布，
哈若西配画。
各色布匹染出了，
泉水洗布布光滑。

从那个时候起，
江边白彝人，
身穿棉布衣，
头包黑纱帕。

Three jin① of each color was bought,
And taken home in a hurry.

De Baixi dyed cloth.
Ha Ruoxi painted.
Cloth in various colors was produced,
Which became smooth after being washed in spring water.

Since then,
Bai Yi people living on riverside,
Wore cotton clothes and
Black headcloth.

① jin: a unit of weight equal to 500 grams.

第二章　绸和缎

泽梗子地方，
有了满五月姑娘，
她第一个知道采桑，
她第一个开始养蚕。

姑娘背着背箩，
每天都爬上高山，
找寻各种叶片片，
采摘回家喂蚕。

走到山头上，
采来绿松针；
走到梁子上，
采来渣拉叶片；
走到大河边，
采来椎栗叶尖。
三种叶子给蚕吃，
蚕儿不吃也不闻。

人不吃饭不能活，
蚕不吃食就会死。

Chapter Two Silks and Satins

In a place named Ze Gengzi,
There is Miss May,
The first one who knew how to gather mulberry leaves,
The first one who knew how to raise silkworms.

The girl carried bamboo basket and
Climbed up to the mountain every day,
Looking for all kinds of leaves,
To take home and feed silkworms.

She came to the mountaintop and,
Picked green pine needles.
She came to the mountain ridge and,
Picked Zala leaves.
She came to the riverside and
Picked leave tips of Huai chestnut.
Three kinds of leaves were fed to silkworms,
But they neither ate nor smelled.

Without food, people cannot live.
Without food, silkworms would die.

满五月姑娘，
又背着箩筐，
四面八方找蚕的饭。

坝中割青草，
河边割藤蔓，
山头采鲜花，
三样东西来喂蚕，
蚕儿还是不吃，
蚕儿还是不咽。

人不吃饭不能活，
蚕不吃食怎吐丝？
满五月姑娘，
再次背背箩上山，
四面八方找蚕的饭。

门前掐来菜叶，
路边扯来柿叶，
山上采来桑叶，
三种叶子倒成三堆，
三种叶子给蚕吃。
菜叶蚕不闻，
柿叶蚕不挨，
桑叶蚕儿吃得喳喳响。
满五月姑娘见了喜欢，
天天采桑叶，
天天仔细看。

Miss May,
Carrying her bamboo basket,
Looked for food for silkworms in all directions.

Grass were cut on the plain.
Vines were cut on the riverside.
Flowers were picked on the mountaintop.
They were fed to silkworms.
Silkworms still did not eat.
Silkworms still did not swallow.

People cannot survive without food.
How could silkworms produce silk if they ate nothing?
Miss May,
Carrying bamboo basket and going up the mountain again,
Looked for food for silkworms in all directions.

Vegetable leaves were pinched off in front of the door.
Persimmon leaves were torn off at the roadside.
Mulberry leaves were picked on the mountain.
Three kinds of leaves were put in three piles.
Three kinds of leaves were fed to silkworms.
Silkworms did not smell vegetable leaves.
Silkworms did not touch persimmon leaves.
Silkworms ate mulberry leaves greedily.
Miss May was so pleased.
She picked mulberry leaves every day and
Observed them carefully every day.

蚕儿吃了桑叶长得快，
蚕儿吐丝啦！
白蚕吐白丝，
黑蚕吐黑丝，
绿蚕吐绿丝，
红蚕吐红丝。
黄蚕吐黄丝。
五样颜色的蚕，
吐出五种丝。

收得蚕丝怎么缫？
收得蚕丝怎么办？
列贵挨姑娘说：
“蚕丝我会缫。”

她有四个好伙伴：
一个峨阿拉姑娘，
一个峨奇俐姑娘，
一个峨夺白姑娘，
一个峨佐作姑娘，
她们四个会缫丝。

白丝缫成堆，
缫得八千团；
黑丝缫成堆，
缫得九千团；
绿丝缫成堆，
缫得八千团；

Silkworms ate mulberry leaves and grew fast.
Silkworms started producing silk!
White silkworms produced white silk.
Black silkworms produced black silk.
Green silkworms produced green silk.
Red silkworms produced red silk.
Yellow silkworms produced yellow silk.
Silkworms in five colors,
Produced cocoons in five different colors.

How to reel silk from cocoons?
How to deal with the cocoon fiber?
Miss Lie Guiai said:
"I know how to reel silk from cocoons."

She had four good friends:
One was Miss E Ala.
One was Miss E Qili.
One was Miss E Duobai.
One was Miss E Zuozuo.
These four girls knew how to reel silk from cocoons.

White silk was reeled into piles.
Eight thousand rolls were got.
Black silk was reeled into piles.
Nine thousand rolls were got.
Green silk was reeled into piles.
Eight thousand rolls were got.

红丝缫成堆，
缫得九千团；
黄丝缫成堆，
缫得八千团。
缫得一百二十堆，
堆满九屋十八院。

列贵挨姑娘真能干，
领头缫丝织绸缎。
六个姑娘十二只手，
织的绸缎数不完。

绸缎织出来了，
还得染绸缎，
不染无色彩，
不染不好看。
哪个找染料？
哪个会染绸缎？

歇索的三个儿子，
都是找虎的好汉。
他们三个齐声说：
“要找颜料不用愁，
要染绸缎不费难。”

他们背着金弓银弩，
他们带上金箭银箭，

Red silk was reeled into piles.
Nine thousand rolls were got.
Yellow silk was reeled into piles.
Eight thousand rolls were got.
Silk was reeled into one hundred twenty piles.
Nine houses and eighteen courtyards were stacked with silk rolls.

Lie Guiai was a capable girl.
She took the lead to reel silk and weave silks and satins.
Six girls with twelve hands,
Produced countless silks and satins.

After the production of silks and satins,
Next step was to dye them.
There was no color before dyeing.
It was not beautiful before dyeing.
Who can find dyes?
Who can dye silks and satins?

Three sons of Xie Suo,
Are good tiger hunters.
They answered together:
"Don't worry about finding dyes.
It's easy to dye silks and satins."

They carried gold bow and silver crossbow.
They carried gold arrows and silver arrows.

领着黑狗白狗，
天天打虎撵山。

他们四处寻找，
找遍了七十七条箐，
寻遍了九十九道湾，
搜遍了一百二十个峰峦，
才找到了老虎的脚印。

歇索的三个儿子，
放出黑狗白狗
拉满金弓银弩，
搭上金箭银箭。
一个山顶滚石头，
两个挡住虎路口。

老虎出来了，
金弓放一箭，
从老虎头上飞过；
银弩放一箭，
从老虎脚下飞过；
金弓银弩一齐放，
箭穿老虎的肋骨，
射中老虎的心肝。
大哥二哥抬老虎，
三弟背弩箭。
老虎抬到家，

Accompanied by black dog and white dog,
They searched the mountain for tigers every day.

They scouted around.
They searched seventy-seven bamboo groves,
Explored ninety-nine coves,
Climbed one hundred and twenty mountains and
Finally found the tiger's footprints.

The three sons of Xie Suo,
Unleashed the black dog and white dog,
Drew full gold bow and silver crossbow and
Fitted the gold arrow and silver arrow.
One of them rolled down a rock from the mountaintop.
The other two barred the tiger's way out.

The tiger came out.
The gold arrow was released,
Flying over the tiger's head.
The silver crossbow was released,
Flying through the tiger's legs.
Th gold bow and silver crossbow were released at the same time.
The arrows penetrated through tiger's ribs and,
Hit the tiger's heart.
Big brother and second brother lifted the tiger.
Third brother carried bows and arrows on his back.
The tiger was carried home.

用金刀剥下老虎皮，
用银刀剖开虎心肝，
挖出护心血，
取出胸中胆，
送给姑娘们染绸缎。

六个姑娘接过护心血，
六个姑娘收下老虎胆，
她们晚上织绸缎，
白天染绸缎，
绸缎染得红彤彤，
绸缎染得光闪闪。

染了又再画，
样样画齐全。
画上月亮和太阳，
画上大地和蓝天。
星宿也画上，
画上片片云彩；
风雨也画上，
画出锦绣山川；
老虎豹子也画上，
马鹿麂子画齐全；
山鸡箐鸡也画上，
红雀绿雀山鹰喜鹊画得展翅飞云端；
庄稼树木也画上，
还画上牲畜和人烟……

The fur was cut with gold knife.
The heart was cut open with silver knife.
The heart blood was dug out.
The gallbladder was taken out.
The blood and the gallbladder were given to girls to dye silks and satins.

Six girls took over heart blood.
Six girls took over tiger's gallbladder.
They weaved silks and satins at night and
Dyed them in the daytime.
Silks and satins were dyed bright red.
Silks and satins were dyed sparkling.

Everything in the world,
Were painted on dyed silks and satins.
The moon and the sun were painted.
The earth and the blue sky were painted.
Constellations were painted.
Cloud clusters were painted.
Wind and rain were painted.
Beautiful landscape was painted.
Tigers and leopards were painted.
Red deer and muntjac were painted,
Pheasant and Qing chicken were painted.
Flying red and green sparrows, eagles, and magpies in clouds,
Crops and trees,
Cattle and households were all painted on silks and satins...

染也染过了，
画也画过了，
还要洗来还要漂，
漂过洗过才美观。

漂洗绸缎没有水，
六个姑娘找水源，
她们走过八十个坝子，
经过八十八座高山；
山下有龙潭，
潭里流清泉，
清泉水好染绸缎。

六个姑娘来挑水，
六个姑娘挑六担；
三担水洗绸，
三挑水漂缎，
绸缎洗得像月亮，
绸缎染得颜色鲜。

绸缎漂好哪里晒？
拿到城里去晒干。
挑着绸缎回到泽梗子，
四道城门大大开，
人出人进像蚂蚁一般。

城墙上晒红绸子，
城楼上晒黄缎子，

Dyeing was finished.
Painting was finished.
Washing and bleaching would be next steps,
Which were indispensable for the beauty of silks and satins.

Washing and bleaching need water.
Six girls went to look for water source.
They walked through eighty plains.
They climbed over eighty-eight high mountains.
The Dragon spring was at the foot of a mountain.
Clear springwater was running and splashing.
Clear springwater was fit for dyeing silks and satins.

Six girls carried water with shoulder poles.
Six girls carried six loads of water.
Three loads were used to wash silks.
Three loads were used to bleach satins.
Silks and satins were washed as bright as moon.
Silks and satins were dyed colorful.

Where to dry them after being bleached?
Dry them in the town.
Silks and satins were carried back to Ze Gengzi.
Four city gates were widely open.
People went in and out just as ants.

Red silks were hung out on ramparts.
Yellow satins were hung out on city towers.

城墙上一片红，
城楼上一片黄。

皇帝见了动心，
都府见了红眼，
县官见了笑成泥一团。
姑娘做成的绸缎，
他们要先拿，
他们要先用。
他们要先穿。

后代的子孙呵，
穿上绸和缎；
莫忘了打虎的兄弟，
莫忘了满五月姑娘采桑养蚕。

Ramparts were all in red.
City towers were all in yellow.

Seeing the silks and satins on ramparts and city towers,
The emperor was enthralled.
Officers were envious.
County magistrates laughed with great delight.
After girls finished producing silks and satins,
They would like to take them first.
They would like to use them first.
They would like to put them on first.

Hey, the offspring,
Wearing silks and satins,
Don't forget the brothers who caught the tiger;
Don't forget Miss May who picked mulberry leaves and fed silkworms.

第三章　金银铜铁锡

泽梗子地方，
黑夺方地方，
有一家两兄弟，
哥哥叫萨阿勒，
弟弟叫西阿德，
阿勒阿德两兄弟，
他们认得藏金银的地方，
他们知道藏铜铁的地方。

三星还没有落，
两兄弟就起床，
鸡叫忙煮饭，
天亮上山冈，
去找金银铜铁锡。
他们走啊走，
走到可叶山上。
山脚细细瞧，
山腰细细找，
看见一大棵金树。
树干黄澄澄，

Chapter Three Gold, Silver, Copper, Iron and Tin

In the place Ze Gengzi,
In the place Hei Duofang,
There were two brothers in a family.
The elder brother's name was Sa Ale.
The younger brother's name was Xi Ade.
Ale and Ade are two brothers.
They knew the place where gold and silver were buried.
They knew the place where copper and iron were buried.

Before three stars faded,
The two brothers got up.
Breakfast was cooked when cock crowed at dawn.
They went up the mountain at daybreak,
To look for gold, silver, cooper, iron and tin.
They went on and on,
Coming to Keye Mountain.
They looked through carefully the foot of the mountain,
And the mountainside.
They saw a gold tree,
With golden tree trunk,

树叶放金光，
树花晶晶亮。
阿勒阿德两兄弟，
心中喜洋洋。
两人齐声说：
“挖开金山采金矿。”

他们继续往前走，
走到峨倮山梁。
山腰细细瞧，
山脚细细找，
看见一大棵银树。
树叶白生生，
树花亮堂堂。
阿勒阿德两兄弟，
脸上笑眯眯。
两人齐声说：
“挖开银山采银矿。”

他们继续往前走，
走到过倮山梁。
山脚细细瞧，
山腰细细找，
看见一棵桐树明晃晃。
满树红彤彤，
树叶亮堂堂，
阿勒阿德兄弟俩，
心头乐滋滋。
两人齐声说：

Glittering leaves and
Sparkling flowers.
The two brothers Ale and Ade
Rejoiced in heart,
Announced together:
"Excavate the gold mountain and strike gold!"

They kept on walking forwards,
Coming to Eluo mountain ridge.
They looked through carefully the mountainside,
And the foot of the mountain.
They saw a silver tree,
With shinning white leaves,
And sparkling flowers.
The two brothers Ale and Ade,
With a smile on their faces,
Announced together:
"Excavate the silver mountain and strike silver!"

They kept on walking forwards,
Coming to Guoluo mountain ridge.
They looked through carefully the foot of the mountain,
And the mountainside.
They saw a gleaming copper tree,
All in bright red,
With shinning leaves.
The two brothers Ale and Ade,
Pleased in heart,
Announced together:

"挖开铜山采铜矿。"

他们继续往前走，
走到纳铁山梁。
山脚细细看，
山腰细细找，
看见一棵大铁树；
树干黑黝黝。
树叶嫩汪汪。
阿勒阿德兄弟俩，
心头好喜欢。
两人齐声说：
"挖开铁山采铁矿。"

他们继续往前走，
直到过梗山梁。
山脚细细瞧，
山腰细细找，
看见一棵大锡树。
锡树白花花，
树叶放白光。
阿勒阿德兄弟俩，
嘴上笑眯眯。
两人齐声说：
"挖开锡山采锡矿。"

兄弟俩走遍五座大山，
找到了埋在山中的宝藏。

"Excavate the copper mountain and strike copper."

They kept on walking forwards,
Coming to Natie mountain ridge.
They looked through carefully the foot of the mountain,
And the mountainside.
They saw a big iron tree,
With shiny black trunk and
Tender leaves.
The two brothers Ale and Ade,
Joyful,
Announced together:
"Excavate the iron mountain and strike iron!"

They kept on walking forwards,
Coming to Guogeng mountain ridge.
They looked through carefully the foot of the mountain,
And the mountainside.
They saw a big tin tree,
In shinning white,
With leaves emitting white light.
The two brothers Ale and Ade,
Beaming with pleasure,
Announced together:
"Excavate the tin mountain and strike tin!"

Going over five mountains,
The brothers found the treasure buried in mountains.

他们要挖出金石头，
挖出银石头，
挖出铜石头，
挖出铁石头，
挖出锡石头，
挖出五种矿。

金银铜铁锡，
五种矿石五个样，
可惜没有水洗，
矿石难放光。

阿勒阿德两兄弟，
到处去找水。
走到文依地方，
找到一股水；
走到赛铁梗邹地方，
找到两股水；
走到塔罗莫科地方，
找到三股水；
走到靖宁梗邹地方，
找到四股水；
走到多别乌井地方，
找到五股水；
走到买迷峨井地方，
找到六股水；
走到文依梭泽地方，
找到七股水；

They dug up gold ore.
They dug up silver ore.
They dug up copper ore.
They dug up iron ore.
They dug up tin ore.
They dug up five types of ores.

Gold, silver, copper, iron and tin,
Five types of ores are different.
There was no water to wash them.
The ores were dim and dark.

The brothers Ale and Ade,
Went to look for water in all places.
Going to a place named Wenyi,
They found a stream.
Going to a place named Saitie Gengzou,
They found two streams.
Going to a place named Taluo Moke,
They found three streams.
Going to a place named Jingning Gengzou,
They found four streams.
Going to a place named Duobie Niaojing,
They found five streams.
Going to a place named Maimi Ejing,
They found six streams.
Going to a place named Wenyi Suoze,
They found seven streams.

走到梁子黑龙水地方，
找到八股水。

两兄弟找到了水，
一齐动手洗矿石。
银石洗得白生生，
金石洗得亮堂堂，
铁石洗得黑黝黝，
铜石洗得明晃晃，
锡石洗得白云样，
样样矿石都放光。

矿石找到了，
矿石洗净了。
可惜没有木炭，
还是不能炼矿。

阿勒阿德两兄弟，
去到峨罗山上，
松树砍了三架山，
柏树砍了十八凹，
栗树砍了九条箐。
他们挖成窑子，
木炭烧出来了。

阿勒阿德两兄弟，
半山砍棵攀枝花枝，
做个大风箱。

Going to a place named Liangzi Heilongshui,
They found eight streams.

The two brothers found water and
Washed the ores together.
Silver ore was washed into shinning white.
Gold ore was washed glittering.
Iron ore was washed into shiny black.
Copper ore was washed gleaming.
Tin ore was washed as white as clouds.
Each ore was glistening.

Ores were found.
Ores were washed.
But without charcoal,
It was impossible to smelt ores.

The brothers Ale and Ade,
Went up the Eluo mountain.
Pine trees on three mountains were cut down.
Cypresses on eighteen mountain ridges were cut down.
Chestnut trees on nine bamboo groves were cut down.
They dug out a kiln.
Charcoal was fired.

The brothers Ale and Ade,
Cut down branches of ceiba on halfway up a mountain,
To make a bellows.

用土基砌个大炉子，
木炭放在正中央，
手拉风箱炉火旺。

阿勒去烧火，
阿德扯风箱，
火光像闪电，
风箱如雷响。
兄弟两个笑眯眯，
流着汗珠炼出矿。

哪个来打金锭银锭？
哪个来打金银首饰？
哪个来打锄头镰刀？
哪个来打茶壶铃铛？

泽梗子地方，
黑夺方地方，
梗郭的三个儿子，
他们白天炼金，
他们晚上铸银，
金块炼成金锭，
银块铸成银锭。
他们白天打金，
他们晚上打银。
金子打成金首饰，
银子打成银首饰。
他们白天炼铜，

A big furnace with mud was built.
Charcoal was put in the middle of the furnace.
The bellows was pulled with hand and fire burnt fiercely.

Ale made a fire.
Ade blew the bellows.
Flames flicked as lightning.
The bellows cracked like thunder.
Two brothers smiled.
They sweated and refined ores.

Who can hammer gold ingots and silver ingots?
Who can make gold and silver jewelry?
Who can forge hoes and sickles?
Who can make teapots and bells?

In the place named Ze Gengzi,
In the place named Hei Duofang,
The three sons of Geng Guo,
Smelted gold ore in the daytime,
And silver ore at night.
Gold nuggets were smelted into gold ingots.
Silver nuggets were smelted into silver ingots.
They forged gold in the daytime.
They forged silver at night.
Gold was forged into gold jewelry.
Silver was forged into silver jewelry.
They smelted copper in the daytime.

他们晚上打铁，
用铜铁做成铜壶、铜盆，
用铁打成锄头镰刀，
用锡铅做成各种用具。

泽梗子地方，
黑夺方地方，
是出金银的地方，
是使用金银的地方。
十斤和五斤，
十两和五两，
不足一斤不使，
不足一两不用。

泽梗子地方嫁囡，
使金使银很平常；
黑夺方地方讨亲，
使金使银很大方；
世上死了人，
使金用银办丧葬；
泽梗子地方的小姑娘，
戴金戴银闪闪亮；
黑夺方地方的小伙子，
戴金戴银人夸奖；

They smelted iron at night.
Copper was forged into kettles and basins.
Iron was forged into hoes and sickles.
Tin and lead were forged into various wares.

The place named Ze Gengzi,
The place named Hei Duofang,
Was the origin of gold and silver and
Was the place gold and silver were used.
Ten jin① and five jin,
Ten liang② and five liang,
Gold or silver,
Whose weight was less than one jin or one liang,
Were out of circulation.

In the marriage of daughters in Ze Gengzi,
It is common to use gold and silver.
In the marriage of sons in Hei Duofang,
Parents were generous with their gold and silver.
When people died,
They used gold and silver to pay for funeral cost.
Young girls in Ze Gengzi,
Wore gold and silver bling.
Young man in Hei Duofang,
Wore gold and silver to win respect.

---

① jin: a unit of weight equal to 500 grams.
② liang: a unit of weight equal to 50 grams.

在他们身上，
金子银子亮晃晃，
金银首饰响叮当。

梗郭的三个儿子，
造出工具千万样。
锄头镰刀有了，
用具什物有了，
世上需要的东西，
样样都造出来了。

On their body,
Gold and silver were glittering.
Gold and silver jewels were clinking.

Three sons of Geng Guo,
Created thousands of different tools.
Hoes and sickles were available.
All kinds of wares were available.
All the tools that were needed in the world,
Had been produced.

第四章 纸和笔

纸用什么造成的？
笔用什么造成的？
纸用树皮造成的，
笔用竹子麝毛造成的。
什么人先造纸？
什么人先造笔？
这是很古的事情，
样样都有来历。

歇索大山上，
歇阿乌最先说：
“我们要写字，
没有纸和笔。”

歇索的三个儿子，
跟着歇阿乌，
白天去找做纸的树皮，
晚上去找做笔的竹枝。

找到东方去，
遇着老绿龙。

Chapter Four　Paper and Pens

What was paper made from?
What was pen made of?
Paper was made from tree bark.
Pen was made of bamboo and musk deer hair.
Who made paper first?
Who made pen first?
It happened thousands of years ago.
Each one had a long history.

On mountain Xie Suo,
Xie Awu said first:
"We want to write,
But there is no paper or pen."

The three sons of Xie Suo,
Followed Xie Awu,
To look for tree bark for making paper in the daytime and
To look for bamboo for making pens at night.

Searching in the east,
They met an old green dragon.

歇阿乌请求它：
“东方是你管理，
这里算你强，
有没有竹子？
有没有造纸的树皮？”
老绿龙回答说：
“东方绿城是我管理，
我没有竹子，
我没有造纸的树皮。”

找到南方去，
遇着老白龙。
歇阿乌请求它：
“南方是你管理，
这里算你有本事，
有没有竹子？
有没有树皮？”
老白龙回答说：
“南方白城是我的属地，
竹子我没有，
树皮我没有。”

找到北方去，
遇着老黑龙，
歇阿乌请求它：
“北方属你管理，
这里数你第一，
有没有竹子？

Xie Awu asked:
"The east is under your supervision.
You are the highest authority.
Do you have bamboo?
Do you have tree bark for making paper?"
The old green dragon answered:
"The eastern green city is under my supervision.
I have no bamboo.
I have no tree bark for making paper."

Searching in the south,
They met an old white dragon.
Xie Awu asked:
"The south is under your supervision.
You are the highest authority.
Do you have bamboo?
Do you have tree bark?"
The old white dragon answered:
"The south white city is under my supervision.
I have no bamboo.
I have no tree bark."

Searching in the north,
They met an old black dragon.
Xie Awu asked:
"The north is under your supervision.
You are the highest authority.
Do you have bamboo?

有没有树皮？”
老黑龙回答说：
“北方黑城是我管理，
我没有竹子，
我没有树皮。”

找到西方去，
遇着老红龙，
歇阿乌请求它：
“西方属你管理，
西方数你第一，
有没有竹子？
有没有树皮？”
老红龙回答说：
“西方红城是我管，
我没有竹子，
我没有树皮。”

歇索的三个儿子，
跟着歇阿乌，
带上金弓银弩，
领着猎狗，
钻进老箐里。

歇阿乌吹牛角，
猎狗汪汪叫。
撵出一对豹子，
穿的铜钱花衣，

Do you have tree bark?"
The old black dragon answered:
"The north black city is under my supervision.
I have no bamboo.
I have no tree bark."

Searching in the west,
They met an old red dragon.
Xie Awu asked:
"The west is under your supervision.
You are the highest authority.
Do you have bamboo?
Do you have tree bark?"
The old red dragon answered:
"The west red city is under my supervision.
I have no bamboo.
I have no tree bark."

The three sons of Xie Suo,
Following Xie Awu,
Carrying gold bow and silver crossbow and
Taking the hound,
Dived into the old bamboo grove.

Xie Awu blew ox horn.
The hound barked.
A pair of leopards were driven out,
With a pattern of copper coin on their fur.

撵出一对老虎，
穿着镰刀花衣。

歇阿乌搭上银箭，
射到半天空，
云彩被打散。
再放第二箭，
射到山肚里，
山崩塌一半。
射不中虎豹，
箭头也不见。

歇索的三个儿子，
跟着歇阿乌，
继续往前走。
猎狗进箐，
牛角吹响；
出来一对马鹿，
穿的红彤彤，
出来一对野猪，
穿的黑黝黝。

歇阿乌拉起银弩，
射到半空中，
天空红一半；
再一箭射到地上，
地炸起一块，
冒起一股尘烟。

A pair of tigers were driven out,
With a pattern of sickle on their fur.

Nocking the silver arrow,
Xie Awu shot the arrow into the air,
Scattering clouds in the sky.
He shot the second arrow,
Which was launched onto the mountainside,
Leading half of the mountain collapse.
The arrow missed the tigers and leopards and
The arrowhead was gone.

The three sons of Xie Suo,
Following Xie Awu,
Kept on walking forwards.
The hound ran into the bamboo grove.
Ox horn was blown.
A pair of red deer came out,
covered with red fur.
A pair of boar came out,
covered with black fur.

Drawing sliver crossbow,
Xie Awu shot the arrow into the air.
Half of the sky turned into red.
The second arrow shooting on the ground,
The ground was blasted into pieces.
A cloud of dust rose.

箭头不见了，
没射中野猪、马鹿。
他们继续往前赶，
心中起疑团。

牛角吹响了，
猎狗钻进深山；
撵出黑漆漆的一对山驴，
撵出灰仆仆的一对岩羊。
歇阿乌搭上银箭，
箭飞上天，
天白一片。
又放一箭，
箭钻进树，
三棵大树被射断。

射不中山驴、岩羊，
难不倒歇阿乌。
又把猎狗放进孟吾大山①，
两边喊哦嚯！
牛角嘟嘟响。
撵出一只麝子。
他们搭上银箭，
箭飞上天，
降下一阵猛雨；

① 孟吾大山：地名。

Arrowhead was gone.
It missed the boar and red deer.
They went on their way.
An impulse of suspicion sprang up in their mind.

Ox horn was blown.
The hound ran into remote mountains.
A pair of black mountain mules was driven out.
A pair of ashy blue sheep was driven out.
Nocking the silver arrow,
Xie Awu shot the arrow into the air.
The sky turned into white.
The second arrow
Shooting into trees,
Three big trees were shot off.

The arrow missed mountain mules and blue sheep.
But Xie Awu was never put off by difficulties.
He sent the hound into Mengwu mountain①,
And shouted "oho" on both sides.
Ox horn tooted.
A musk deer was driven out.
Nocking the silver arrow,
He shot the arrow into the air.
Rain poured for a while.

---

① Mengwu mountain: name of a place.

又放一箭，
箭钻进地，
地冒一股水。
雨停河水涨，
淌出一枝金箭来。

歇阿乌拉起银弩，
歇阿乌搭上金箭，
射到麝子的肋巴里，
麝子倒毙。

歇索的三个儿子，
把麝子抬回家里，
歇阿乌剖开麝头，
麝头没有脑浆，
却有三颗竹子种，
有三颗纸树籽。
挖开麝心，
麝子心中没有血，
却有三颗竹子种，
有三颗纸树籽。
敲开麝骨头，
不见有骨髓，
却有三颗竹子种，
有三颗纸树籽。

歇索的三个儿子，
跟着歇阿乌，

The second arrow
Was shot into the earth.
A spout of water came out.
The rain stopped and the river swelled.
A gold arrow flowed out from the river.

Xie Awu drew sliver crossbow.
Xie Awu nocked the gold arrow.
He shot at the ribs of the musk deer.
The musk deer dropped dead.

The three sons of Xie Suo,
Carried the musk deer back home.
Xie Awu cut open its head.
There were no brains in it,
But three bamboo seeds
And three paper tree seeds.
Xie Awu cut open its heart.
There was no blood,
But three bamboo seeds,
And three paper tree seeds.
Xie Awu knocked open its bone.
There was no marrow,
But three bamboo seeds
And three paper tree seeds.

The three sons of Xie Suo,
Followed Xie Awu.

砍出三块地，
放火来烧地，
烧出草灰种纸树。

竹子种撒满山坡，
纸树籽撒在地里，
竹子绿茵茵，
纸树露白皮。

歇索的三个儿子，
跟着歇阿乌，
银刀别腰上，
砍回三捆竹子，
砍回三捆纸树，
砍倒三棵青冈树，
做成打纸棒，
背回一个大石滚，
用石滚来碾纸。

歇阿乌的阿妈，
白天打纸，
晚上打纸，
竹子做笔管，
麝毛做笔头，
做成纸和笔。

They slashed three piece of field and
Burnt them.
The burnt ash was used to plant paper trees.

Bamboo seeds were scattered all over the mountainside.
Paper tree seeds were scattered on the earth.
Verdant bamboo grew.
Paper trees revealed its white bark.

The three sons of Xie Suo,
Followed Xie Awu.
Silver knives were stuck on waist.
Three bales of bamboo were cut and taken back.
Three bales of paper trees were cut and taken back.
Three bales of oriental white oaks were cut down.
A paper-striking stick was made from them.
A big stone wheel was carried home
To roll paper.

Xie Awu's mother,
Produced paper at the daytime,
And at night.
The shaft of pen was made of bamboo.
The end of pen was made of musk deer hair.
Paper and pens were finished.

笔有了，
纸也有了，
一百二十个老师，
不分热天和冷天，
不管风季和雨季，
让彝家子子孙孙读书写字。

They got pens.
They got paper.
One hundred and twenty teachers,
No matter in summer or winter,
No matter it was windy or rainy,
Taught the offspring of Yi people to read and write.

第五章　书

泽梗子地方，
有三条河谷，
有三座高山，
住着三个伙伴。
一个叫赛季考叶莫，
一个叫倮佐赛叶勒，
一个叫多倮勒文莫。
三人齐撒种，
树种撒得多，
遍地树花数不清。
阿朴独姆西嘛，
树木名字不晓得，
山川名字不会分……

黑夺方地方，
山梁有三个，
大坝有三个。
山梁上的竹子绿茵茵，

Chapter Five Books

In the place named Ze Gengzi,
There were three valleys.
There were three mountains.
Three guys lived there.
One was Saiji Kaoyemo.
One was Luozuo Saiyele.
Another one was Duoluo Lewenmo.
They scattered seeds together,
Most of which were tree seeds.
There were countless trees and flowers all over the ground.
Apu Dumuxi, hey,
Could not tell the difference,
Of various trees or,
Of various mountains...

In the place named Hei Duofang,
There were three mountain ridges and
There were three plains.
The bamboos on mountain ridges were shiny green.

山梁上的藤子满坡生。
坝子的青草绿又嫩，
坝子里的海水明如镜。
阿朴独姆西嘛，
竹子藤子不晓得，
大海小海不会分，
年月节令也分不清。

涅依撒萨歇，
百事都关心，
把人间的难事，
找罗阿玛询问。

龙王罗阿玛，
昼夜画图写书文。
天地日月画出来，
草木风雨画出来，
粮食种子画出来，
马鹿野兽画出来，
男人女人画出来……
阿朴独姆西也画出来，
世上万物一齐画出来。

画成万物十二册，
写成字书十二本。
有本有篇又有了行，
样样画得清，
事理写得明。

The vines on mountain ridges extended all over the mountainsides
Grasses on plains were in light green.
Water in plains was bright as a mirror.
Apu Dumuxi, hey,
Did not know bamboos or vines,
Did not know big water or small water, and
Could not tell the difference between the year, the month and festivals.

Nienong Sashaxie,
Cared about everything.
He brought the difficulties in the world,
To Luo Ama for answer.

Dragon Queen Luo Ama,
Drew pictures and wrote articles days and nights.
The sky, the earth, the sun and the moon were drawn.
Grasses, trees, wind and rain were drawn.
Grains and seeds were drawn.
Red deer and wild animals were drawn.
Men and women were drawn...
Apu Dumuxi was drawn too.
Everything on the world was drawn.

Twelve volumes of pictures were finished.
Twelve books of characters were done.
Everything was put into lines, chapters, and books.
Everything was drawn vividly in pictures.
Principles were illustrated clearly.

龙王罗阿玛，
向黑夺方丢下画图来，
向泽梗子丢下书文来，
把图画和书文送给人间。

阿朴独姆西拾起字书，
翻了又翻，
吟了又吟。
白天学书上的画。
夜晚学书上的文。
书上的字学会了，
书上的道理懂得了，
万事万物也会分了。

天气冷一回，
就是一年啰，
年大十三月，
年小十二月；
月亮圆一回，
就是一月啰，
月大三十天，
月小二十九天；
十四、十五月亮圆，
十六、十七月更明；
年月大小书上有，
日子长短书上写得清，

Dragon Queen Luo Ama,
Threw the pictures in Hei Duofang and
Threw the books in Ze Gengzi.
He sent pictures and books to human beings.

Apu Dumuxi picked up the books,
Turned the books page by page, and
Read the books again and again.
He studied the pictures in books in the daytime.
He studies the characters in books at night.
He learned characters in the books,
Learned to understand the principles in the books, and
To distinguish everything on the earth.

Once the weather turned cold,
One year passed.
There were thirteen months in a leap year.
There were twelve months in a year.
Well, full moon appeared once,
In a month.
There were thirty days in a big month.
There were twenty-nine days in a small month.

Moon turned full on the fourteenth and fifteenth dates of the month.

Moon turned brighter on the sixteenth and seventeenth dates of the month.

The length of years and months were recorded in the books.

The length of days were recorded clearly in the books.

天干地支书上写得明。

阿朴独姆西，
喊来儿子和姑娘，
告诉书上的道理：
莫忘老古根，
莫忘老书文。

这些书是祖先拾得的，
这些书是祖先写下的，
它是阿朴独姆西一代一代传下来的。
没有这些书，
万物名字咋记清？
你说罗阿玛大，
我说涅依倮佐颇更大，
天地和万物，
是他们创造的。
他们的功劳载书上，
他们的功劳万古存。

他说天地大，
我说天地不算大，
天地的名字自己不会取，
天地的名字要人来取，
要是没有书，
名字谁来记？

Ten Heavenly Stems and Twelve Earthly Branches were recorded clearly in the books.

Apu Dumuxi,
Asked his sons and daughters to come,
And taught them the principles in the books:
Don't forget the origin.
Don't forget the ancient books.

These books were kept by ancestors.
These books were written by ancestors.
They were passed down by Apu Dumuxi generation after generation.
Without these books,
Everything in the world would be confusing.
You said Luo Ama was powerful.
I said Nienong Luozuopo was more powerful.
The heavens, the earth and everything
Were created by them.
Their contribution was recorded in books.
Their contribution would be remembered forever.

He said the heavens and the earth were mighty.
I said the heavens and the earth were not mighty enough.
The heavens and the earth cannot be named by themselves.
The heavens and the earth should be named by humans.
If there was no book,
How could the names be recorded?

你说日月星宿大，
我说日月星宿大，
日月星宿不算大；
日月星宿的名字自己不会取，
日月星宿的名字人来取，
取了名字记书上。
要是没有书，
名字不会有。

你说天王地王大，
我说天王地王大，
天王管着日月星辰，
地王管着世上万物。
天王地王不算大，
天王地王的名字自己不会取，
天王地王的名字人来取，
取了名字记书上。
要是没有书，
名字不会有。

你说独眼睛人大，
我说独眼睛人大；
你说直眼睛人大，
我说直眼睛人大；
你说横眼睛人大，
我说横眼睛人大；
独眼睛人的时代没有书，

You said the sun, the moon and the stars were mighty.
I said the sun, the moon and the stars were mighty.
The sun, the moon and the stars were not mighty enough.
They cannot be named by themselves.
They should be named by humans.
The names were recorded in books.
If there had been no book,
Names would have been lost.

You said the heaven king and the earth king were mighty.
I said the heaven king and the earth king were mighty.
The heaven king was in charge of the sun, the moon and the stars.
The earth king was in charge of everything on the earth.
The heaven king and the earth king were not mighty enough.
They cannot be named by themselves.
They should be named by humans.
The names were recorded in books.
If there had been no book,
Names would have been lost.

You said one-eyed person was mighty.
I said one-eyed person was mighty.
You said vertical-eyed person was mighty.
I said vertical-eyed person was mighty.
You said horizontal-eyed person was mighty,
I said horizontal-eyed person was mighty.
There was no book in the era of one-eyed person.

独眼睛人的名字自己不会取；
直眼睛人的时代没有书，
直眼睛人的名字自己不会取。
横眼睛人的时代没有书，
横眼睛人的名字自己不会取。
独眼睛人的名字，
直眼睛人的名字，
横眼睛人的名字，
都是后代人来取，
他们还是不算大。
我说天上的娑罗树大，
娑罗树长在月亮里，
娑罗树千年不会死。
娑罗树不算大，
娑罗树的名字自己不会取，
娑罗树的名字人来取，
取了名字记书上。
要是没有书，
名字不会有。

你说粮食树木大，
要是没有粮食，
阿朴独姆西活不成；
要是没有树木，
鸟兽怎安寝？
粮食树木不算大，
粮食树木不会自己取个名，
粮食树木的名字人来取，

One-eyed person did not know how to name himself.
There was no book in the era of vertical-eyed person.
Vertical-eyed person did not know how to name himself.
There was no book in the era of horizontal-eyed person.
Horizontal eyed person did not know how to name himself.
The name of one-eyed person,
The name of vertical-eyed person,
The name of horizontal-eyed person,
Were all given by their offspring.
They were not mighty enough.
I believed the shorea tree in the sky was mighty.
It lived in the moon,
And was still alive after thousands of years.
The shorea tree was not mighty.
It could not name itself.
It should be named by humans.
The names were recorded in books.
If there had been no book,
The names would have been lost.

You believed grains and trees were mighty.
Without grains,
Apu Dumuxi could not live.
Without trees,
Where were the shelters of birds and wild animals?
Grains and trees are not mighty enough.
They could not name themselves.
They should be named by humans.

取了名字记书上。
要是没有书，
粮食树木难区分。

你说鸟兽大，
鸟兽会唱各样音。
九十架山梁上，
老虎豹子叫，
马鹿麝子鸣；
深沟老箐里，
山鸡野鸡吟；
河边岩子上，
野兔岩羊叫不停；
荆棘刺蓬里，
黑蛇绿蛇哼。
鸟兽不算大，
鸟兽的名字不会自己分，
鸟兽的名字人来取，
取了名字记书上。
书上有鸟兽的名字，
从此鸟兽有大名。

你说山梁子大，
他说山梁子高入云。
三十六架山梁子上，
密布葱葱老林，
山梁上万花红遍，
山梁上果实累累，

The names were recorded in books.
If there had been no book,
Grains and trees would have been hardly distinguishable.

You believed that birds and wild animals were mighty.
Birds and wild animals can produce various sounds.
On the ninety mountain ridges,
Tigers and leopards howled.
Red deer and musk deer barked.
In the deep valleys and old bamboo groves,
Pheasant crowed.
Over the rocks on the riverside,
Hares and blue sheep kept on crying.
In thistles and thorns,
Black and green snakes hissed.
Birds and wild animals were not mighty enough.
They could not name themselves.
They should be named by humans.
The names were recorded in books.
There were names of birds and wild animals in books.
Since then they got formal names.

You believed that mountain ridges were mighty.
He believed that mountain ridges high up into clouds.
The thirty-six mountain ridges,
Were thickly dotted with forests,
Were blanketed with blossoming flowers and
Were covered with fruitful trees.

山梁子不为大，
山梁子不会自己取个名，
山梁子的名字人来取，
山梁名字记书上，
从此山梁天下闻名。

你说坝子大，
他说坝子宽无垠。
三十六个大坝子，
流水潺潺绕坝心；
三十六个大海子，
海里白浪尽翻滚。
老鹰天上转，
白鹤水面飞，
野鸭水中扇翅膀，
大鱼小鱼闪金鳞，
水獭想吃鱼，
常常徘徊在海滨。
坝子、海子不算大，
坝子、海子的名字自己不会取，
坝子、海子的名字人来取。
坝子、海子的名字记书上，
从此坝子、海子有大名。

你说江河大，
他说江河深。
三十六条江，
条条宽又长，

The mountain ridges were not mighty enough.
The mountain ridges could not name themselves.
They should be named by humans.
The names were recorded in books.
Since then they were world-famous.

You believed that plains were mighty.
He believed that plains were boundless.
There were thirty-six great plains,
Across which streams wound their sinuous ways.
There are thirty-six large lakes,
In which whitecaps spat foam.
Eagles circled around in the sky.
White cranes flew over the lake.
Wild ducks fluttered their wings on water.
The scales of fishes of various sizes flashed.
Intending to catch fishes,
Otters wandered about on the lakeside.
Plains and lakes were not mighty enough.
Plains and lakes could not name themselves.
They should be named by humans.
Their names were recorded in books.
Since then they got their formal names.

You believed rivers were mighty.
He believed rivers were deep.
There were thirty-six rivers.
All were wide and long.

条条江水归大海，
条条江水流不尽。
江水不算大，
江水的名字自己不会取，
江水的名字人来取。
江水名字记书上，
从此大江大河有个名。

你说十二样礼节大，
他说十二样礼节难分清。
学会磕头作揖第一样，
分清日月星宿能辨时辰；
学会处人办事第三样，
尊敬爹妈道理明；
分清一年四季第五样，
婚丧嫁娶众遵循；
喜客爱朋彝家礼，
说话恭谨人相亲；
读书求学寻常事，
十二样礼节记在心。
十二样礼节记书上，
规矩、礼节教子孙。

All were going into the sea.
All were flowing with endless water.
Rivers were not mighty enough.
Rivers could not name themselves.
They should be named by humans.
The names were recorded in books.
Since then they got formal names.

You believed the twelve rules of etiquette were important.
He believed the twelve rules of etiquette were indistinguishable.
Showing respect by kowtowing was the first thing to learn.
Observing the sun, the moon and the stars were essential to know time.
Manners of dealing with people and things was the third thing to learn.
Respecting parents was a basic rule.
Distinguishing four seasons was the fifth thing to learn.
Marriage and funeral ceremonies should observe rules.
Welcoming guests and loving friends was the tradition of Yi people.
Being humble increased intimacy between people.
To read and learn were daily activities.
Twelve rules of etiquette were borne in mind.
Twelve rules of etiquette were recorded in books.
Rules and etiquette were passed on to offspring.

世上万物有字书，
世上万物有图画，
万物的名字罗阿玛写出来，
字书是阿朴独姆西传下来，
彝家的规矩是阿朴独姆西教出来。
假若没有阿朴独姆西，
字书谁过问？
假若没有字书，
彝家的道理谁传闻？

Everything in the world was recorded in wordbooks.
Everything in the world was drawn in pictures.
Name of everything was written by Luo Ama.
The wordbooks were handed down by Apu Dumuxi.
Rules of Yi people were taught by Apu Dumuxi.
Without Apu Dumuxi,
Who kept the wordbooks?
Without wordbooks,
Who knew the tradition of Yi people?

第六章　长生不老药

彝家学会开矿藏，
学会种麻粮，
学会织绸缎，
学会养猪羊。
有吃有穿不用愁，
只愁有病咋医治。
只愁有病不死嘛，
还要找寻长生不老药。

彝家有个老阿妈，
名叫拉兵也欧，
三年病魔缠身，
请来西波①叫魂。
祭神送鬼都搞过，
疾病还是不见好；

① 西波：即贝玛，或朵觋。在缺医少药的旧社会，生产力低下，人有了病就请西波念经送鬼。西波识彝文，是彝族的知识分子。

Chapter Six　The Elixir

Yi people learnt to mine,
To plant flax,
To weave silks and satins,
And to raise pigs and sheep.
They did not need to worry about foods and clothes,
But still longed for treatment for illness,
For lifesaving method,
And for the elixir.

There was an old lady,
Whose name was Labing Yeou.
She had been tortured by illness for three years.
Xi Bo① was sent to conjure up spirits.
Sacrifices to gods were offered and the exorcism of demons were carried out,
But the old lady did not recover.

---

① Xi Bo: also called Bei Ma or Duo Xi. In the old society which was short of doctors and medicines and with low productivity, they would invite Xi Bo to recite scriptures to conjure away ghosts when people were sick. Xi Bo can read Yi language. He was an intellectual of the Yi people.

世上药草都吃遍，
要吃长生不老药才会好。

哪个知道长生不老药，
这种药又到哪里找？
拉兵也欧的儿子，
名叫拉兵也欧。
他身披披毡，
头戴篾帽，
骑着马儿去求医，
找来神药救阿妈。

拉兵也欧啊，
翻过千座山，
渡过万条河，
四方都找遍，
问过老少和渔樵，
听说有一个姑娘，
名叫西说阿墨勒，
她认得长生不老药。
拉兵也欧跳下马，
去找西说阿墨勒。

消息传进皇宫里，
皇帝派儿子来抢药。
他们吹着唢呐，
他们敲着锣鼓，

Every herbal medicine had been tried,
But only the elixir can cure her.

Who knew the elixir?
Where could people find it?
The son of Labing Yeou,
Had the same name Labing Yeou.
Wearing a cape,
And a bamboo hat,
He rode on horse to look for a doctor and
To find magical medicine to save the old lady.

Labing Yeou, aha,
Climbed over hundreds of mountains,
Went cross thousands of rivers, and
Searched in all directions,
He asked the old, the young, the fishermen and the woodcutters.
He heard there was a girl,
Whose name was Xishuo Amole.
She knew the elixir.
Labing Yeou jumped off from the horse,
To look for the girl.

The news was passed into imperial palace.
The emperor sent his son to rob the elixir.
They blew Suona.
They beat gongs and drums.

扛着旗子带着兵，
要把长生不老药抢进宫廷。

他们审问西说阿墨勒：
“长生不老药在哪里？
快点交出来！
免挨棍棒打，
免挨坐监牢！
只要交出来，
金银任你抓，
绸缎任你挑！”

西说阿墨勒姑娘，
咬着牙齿叉着腰。
“我什么也没有，
我什么也不知道。”
皇帝的儿子，
等了三夜三朝。
用尽欺哄骇诈，
要了无数花招。
西说阿墨勒姑娘，
就是不交出长生不老药苗。

白树山头上，
有一个牧羊佬，
放着一群绵羊，
羊像白云飘。

They carried flags and led troops,
To rob the elixir into imperial palace.

They interrogated Xishuo Amole:
"Where is the elixir?
Hand it over right now!
Otherwise you will be beaten with sticks,
And be put into jail.
Once you hand it over,
The gold and silver,
The silks and satins,
Are all at your disposal."

Miss Xishuo Amole,
Clenched her teeth and stood with arms akimbo.
"I have nothing.
I have no idea."
The son of the emperor,
Waited for three days and nights.
He tried to cajole and threaten,
And played countless other tricks.
Miss Xishuo Amole,
Refused to hand over the elixir.

On the top of White Tree mountain,
There was a shepherd,
Herding a group of sheep,
which were like floating clouds.

牧羊佬晚上数羊，
一只大公羊不见了。
第二天清早，
三个牧羊人，
带着猎狗四处找，
走遍大山小箐，
寻遍深山林坳，
都没有把羊子找到。

三个牧羊人，
来到荒山坳。
看见公羊倒在大树旁，
原来公羊吃了草乌叶①，
嘴里吐白沫，
不动也不叫。

三个牧羊人，
围着大公羊落泪，
围着大公羊悲伤。
西说阿墨勒姑娘，
突然来到荒山坳。
她拿出仙药敲敲羊头，
羊头抬起来了；
她用药敲敲羊脚，

① 草乌：一种野生药材，毒性很大。

The shepherd counted the number of sheep at night.
He found a big ram gone.
In the morning of the next day,
Three shepherds,
Took their hounds and searched in all directions.
They went over high mountains and little bamboo groves.
They climbed over remote mountains and searched the woods.
But they could not find the ram.

The three shepherds,
Came to a barren mountain col,
And found the ram fell down beside a big tree.
After eating Fohum Aconiti Kusnezoffii①,
The ram frothed at the mouth, and
Remained motionless.

Surrounding the ram,
The three shepherds cried
Sorrowfully.
Miss Xishuo Amole,
Came to the col suddenly.
She took out the elixir and knocked at the head of ram, and
The ram raised its head.
She used the elixir to knock at the feet of ram, and

① Fohum Aconiti Kusnezoffii: a wild herbal medicine which is highly poisonous.

羊脚动起来了；
她再用药敲敲羊身子，
羊就会跑会跳了。

牧羊人又喜又笑，
就向姑娘讨药苗：
“把你的仙药分给我们，
天上星星摘给你，
地上金银随你要。”

姑娘微微笑：
“你们要仙药不难，
回去拿东西来换：
我要白麝的牙齿，
我要世上最好的口弦。”

“口弦身边带得有，
白麝牙齿设法找。”
三个牧羊人告诉拉兵也欧，
忙把公羊往回吆。

拉兵也欧啊，
为了救活阿妈，
下决心去打白麝，
不怕山高路遥。

The ram moved its feet.
She used the elixir to knock at the body of ram, and
The ram began to jump.

The shepherds were happy and smiled.
They asked the girl for the elixir:
"Please give part of your elixir to us,
We will give you the stars in the sky,
And any treasure on the earth."

The girl smiled and said:
"It is not difficult for you to get the elixir.
Go and fetch things to exchange for it.
I want the teeth of white musk deer.
I want the best mouth harp in the world."

"We have the best mouth harp with us,
But we cannot find the teeth of white musk deer."
Three shepherds told Labing Yeou everything,
And loudly urged on their ram back home.

Aha, Labing Yeou,
In order to save the old lady,
Determined to hunt the white musk deer,
Regardless of high mountains and long distance.

他领上十二只猎狗，
抬上十二张猎网，
天不亮就动身，
天黑还不歇脚。
走到大山上，
走到悬崖边，
走到大江畔，
走到小河旁，
走进老林里，
钻进草蓬中，
熬过了无数的白天黑夜，
不见麝子心里焦。

有一天走到山梁上，
看见细沙路上两行脚印，
猎狗闻到麝子味，
对着山梁汪汪咬。
大狗堵中间，
小狗围四方。

只听草在响，
只见草在摇，
一对麝子跑出来，
张嘴露白牙，
抬头四处瞧。

Taking twelve hounds,
Carrying twelve hunting nets,
He started the journey before sunrise, and
Went on with the journey after sunset.
He walked on the mountains,
On the edge of the cliff,
On the riverside,
On the side of streams,
Into thick forest,
And through brushes.
Countless days and nights passed,
He couldn't find the musk deer and felt anxious.

One day walking on the mountain ridge,
He saw two lines of footprint on sandy road.
Catching the smell of musk deer,
The hounds barked at the mountain ridge.
Big hounds blocked the middle way.
Small hounds surrounded them in all directions.

Only grass sounded,
And waved.
A pair of musk deer ran out,
Revealing their white teeth, and
Looking around.

拉兵也欧拉满弓，
一箭射中白麝腿，
白麝滚山腰。
麝肉喂大狗，
麝血喂小狗，
麝香官家要，
麝皮送给西波，
麝牙留着换药苗。

他解下身上的口弦，
他带上麝子的牙齿，
找到西说阿墨勒，
去换长生不老的药苗。

西说阿墨勒姑娘，
一手接口弦，
一手接麝牙，
睁大眼睛仔细瞧。
她告诉拉兵也欧：
“白山头上，
有棵三杈树，
树叶绿茵茵，
树枝分三杈，
树左挖三下，
就能挖到长生不老药苗。”
“还要配上长虫、白麝胆，

Drawing full bow,
Labing Yeou shot at the leg of a musk deer.
The white musk deer rolled down to the mountainside.
The flesh was fed to big hounds.
The blood was fed to small hounds.
The musk was taken away by the government official.
The fur was sent to Xi Bo.
The teeth were kept for exchanging the elixir.

The mouth harp on his body untied,
The musk deer teeth taken,
He found Xishuo Amole,
To exchange for the elixir.

Miss Xishuo Amole,
Took the mouth harp with one hand,
Took the musk deer teeth with the other hand,
Opened her eyes and looked carefully.
She told Labing Yeou:
"On the top of White mountain,
There is a three-branch tree.
The tree leaves are shiny green.
The tree branches into three parts.
Dig for three times on the left side of the ground under the tree,
And you will find the elixir."
"And mix it with snake, musk deer gallbladder,

配上绵羊山羊胆。
要细细地舂，
要透透地熬，
病人吃了就会好，
好人吃了长生不老。”

拉兵也欧啊，
把姑娘的话记牢。
药配好了，
又去问西说阿墨勒姑娘：
“药应该怎样舂？
药又应该怎样熬？”
西说阿墨勒姑娘说：
“你去打只老鹰来，
鹰头做杵臼，
鹰骨做杵棒，
翅膀来扫药，
鹰脚当药盅，
滚沸开水来熬药。”

拉兵也欧把药舂好，
煮药的水到哪里找？
无火怎样把药熬。
西说阿墨勒姑娘说：
“没有水莫着急，
没有火莫心焦，
我到龙王处借水，
我到家中找火苗。”

Sheep gallbladder and goat gallbladder.
Pound them gently.
Stew them thoroughly.
After eating them,
Sick people will recover soon,
Healthy people will be young forever."

Aha, Labing Yeou,
bore the girl's words in mind.
After mixing the drug,
He went to ask Miss Xishuo Amole
"How to pound the drug?
How to stew the drug?"
Miss Xishuo Amole said:"
Go hunt an eagle.
Use eagle's head as the mortar.
Use the eagle's bone as the pestle.
Use the wings to sweep drug.
Use the feet as the drug cup.
Use the boiling water to stew the drug."

Labing Yeou finished pounding the drug.
Where can he find the water for stewing it?
How can he stew the drug without fire?
Miss Xishuo Amole said:
"Don't worry about water.
Don't worry about fire.
I will borrow water from Dragon King.
I will fetch fire at home."

拉兵也欧啊，
样样东西都有啦，
到麻栎树底下，
烧火把药熬。
药气熏上麻栎树，
从此一年换一次叶，
千年万载不会凋。
世上所有的树，
都被药气熏过，
不管雪打雨淋，
不管日晒风吹，
年年都换叶，
年年长新枝。

拉兵也欧把药煮好了，
就是没有搅药的东西，
折枝松椏来搅，
松树沾上药味，
万年长青水不凋。

药汤煮涨了，
忽然一阵风吹过，
药汤熏在杨柳上，
从此倒插杨柳，
插在哪里哪里会生苗。

拉兵也欧嘛，
把煮好的药端给阿妈吃，

Aha, Labing Yeou,
Getting everything he needed,
Lighted fire under the Sawtooth Oak
To stew the drug.
The drug steam bathed the Sawtooth Oak.
Since then the tree grew new leaves once a year.
The tree never withered or fell in thousands of years.
All the trees in the world,
Once bathed in drug steam,
Would change leaves every year,
And grow new branches every year,
No matter it was snowy or rainy,
No matter it was sunny or windy.

Labing Yeou finished stewing the drug,
But did not have tool to stir it.
He broke off the pine tree branch to stir.
The pine tree branch was stuck with the elixir,
Remained green forever and never withered.

The boiling drug soup swelled.
A gust of wind came.
Steam from the drug soup was blown onto willows.
Since then wherever the willow was planted,
It would sprout.

Aha, Labing Yeou,
Took the stewed drug to feed the old lady.

医好了阿妈的病，
阿妈就长生不老。
药罐里还剩点药汤，
请大家都来尝尝。

东方的人吃了，
东方的人永远不会死；
南方的人吃了，
南方的人永远不会死；
西方的人吃了，
西方的人永远不会死；
北方的人吃了，
北方的人永远不会死；
世上的人都吃了，
人人到老都不会死。

鸟雀来吃了，
鸟雀不会死；
野兽来吃了，
野兽不会死；
昆虫来吃了，
昆虫不会死……
吃过长生不老药的飞禽走兽，
熏过长生不老药的花草树木，
千年都活着，
万年不会凋。

The old lady was cured,
And lived forever.
There was some soup left in the drug cup.
Everybody was invited to have a taste.

The easterners ate, and
They would never die.
The southerners ate, and
They would never die.
The westerners ate, and
They would never die.
The northerners ate, and
They would never die.
People on the earth ate, and
Everyone would never die.

Birds came and ate, and
They would never die.
Beast came and ate, and
They would never die.
Insects came and ate, and
They would never die...
The birds and wild animals who ate the elixir,
The vegetation which had been bathed by the elixir,
Would live in the world for thousands of years,
And not wither for tens of thousands of years.

剩下的药没有煮，
剩下的药没有熬，
拿到门外晒一晒，
却被太阳月亮看见了，
太阳月亮跑下来，
偷走了长生不老药。
太阳吃了长生不老药，
太阳永远当空照。
月亮吃了长生不老药，
月亮夜晚望着大地笑。

太阳月亮偷去长生不老药，
大家心头焦。
一齐来商量，
“这药不能丢，
一定要找回这个宝。”

你搬来金柱，
我搬来银柱，
搭成天梯万丈高。
西说阿墨勒姑娘，
拉兵也欧小伙子，
领着一只秃尾虎，
领着一只大黑狗，
上到天宫去要药苗。

The left drug that had not been boiled,
The left drug that had not been stewed,
Was taken out of the house to dry in the sun.
The sun and the moon saw it.
They fell off and,
Stole the elixir.
After eating the drug,
The sun shined in the sky eternally.
After eating the drug,
The moon looked at the earth and smiled at night.

The sun and the moon stole the elixir.
People were worried,
And had a discussion together:
"The drug cannot be lost.
It must be found."

You fetched gold columns.
I fetched silver columns.
They were put up into a sky ladder of ten thousand zhang①.
Miss Xishuo Amole,
The young man Labing Yeou,
Taking a tiger without tail,
And a black dog,
Went up into the heaven palace for the elixir.

---

① zhang: a unit of length equal to 3 and 1/3 meter.

忘记找白蚂蚁商量，
忘记找黄蚂蚁商量，
白蚂蚁咬断了银柱子，
黄蚂蚁咬断了金柱子。
西说阿墨勒姑娘，
拉兵也欧小伙子，
从天上掉下来，
摔死在荒郊。

老虎黑狗最先走了，
老虎黑狗上了天。
老虎要报主人恩，
天天要药苗；
太阳不给它，
它在天上吃太阳；
从此太阳有黑点，
那个老虎啃太阳。
老虎大口啃太阳的时候，
那就是日食。

黑狗要报主人恩，
天天叮着月亮要药苗，
月亮不给它，
它在天上吃月亮。
请看月宫昏暗时，
那是黑狗啃月亮。
黑狗大口吃月时，
那就是月食。

They forgot to have a discussion with white ants.
They forgot to have a discussion with yellow ants.
White ants snapped the silver columns.
Yellow ants snapped the gold columns.
Miss Xishuo Amole and
The young man Labing Yeou,
Fell off from the sky
To die in a desolate area.

The tiger and the black dog ran away in advance.
They went up into heaven.
The tiger wanted to pay the debt of its owner's gratitude.
It asked for the elixir every day.
The sun refused to give.
So the tiger ate the sun in the sky.
Since then there were black spots on the sun,
When the tiger had a bite on it.
When the tiger had a big bite,
The solar eclipse appeared.

The black dog intended to pay the debt of its owner's gratitude,
And asked the moon for the elixir.
The moon refused to give,
So the black dog ate the moon in the sky.
When the black dog was eating the moon,
It turned dim.
When the dog took a big bite,
The lunar eclipse appeared.

彝族的祖先啊，
因为丢了长生不老药，
所以人就会老，
所以人就会死。

The ancestors of Yi people,
Because they lost the elixir,
People would turn old and
People would die.